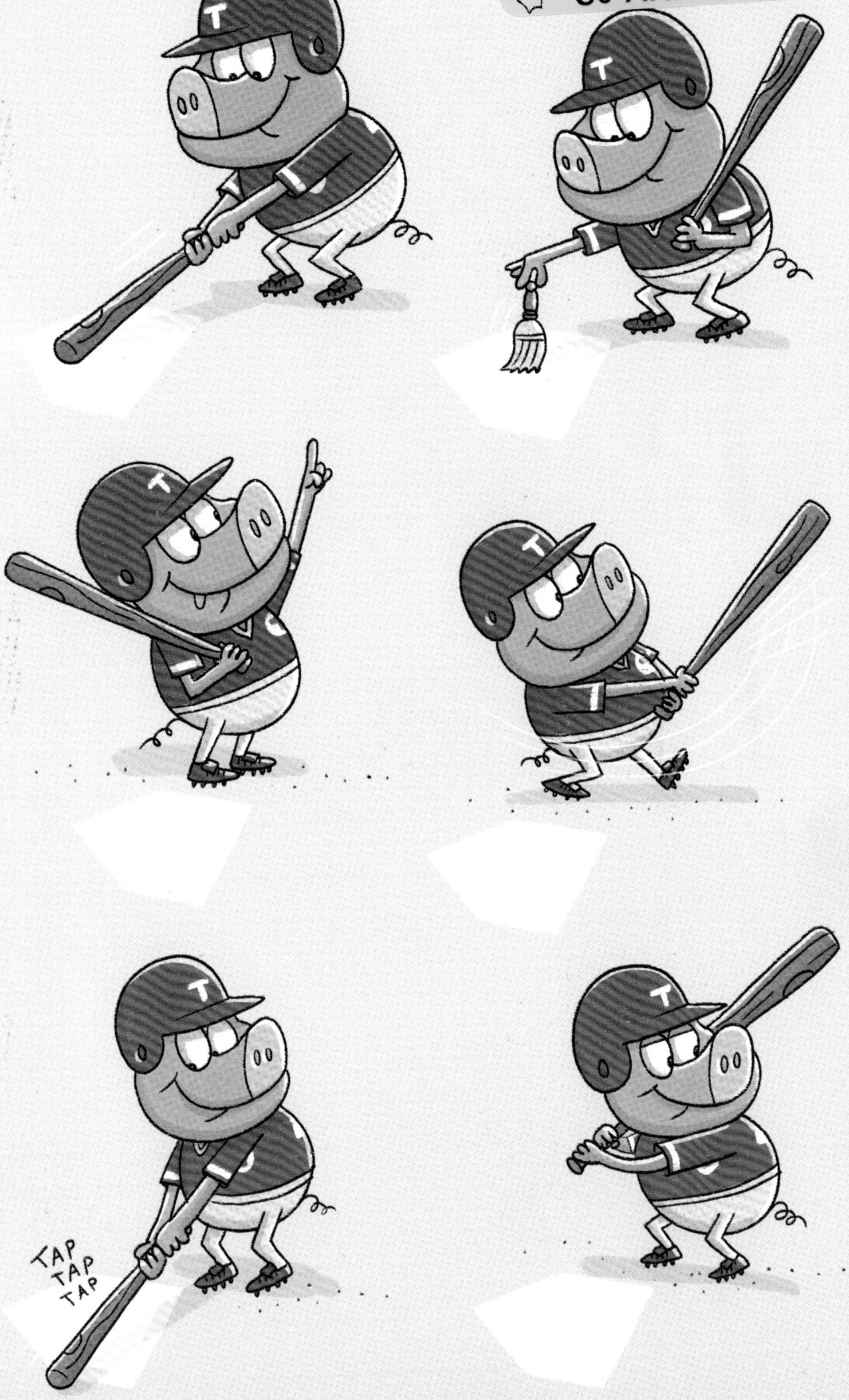
TAP
TAP
TAP

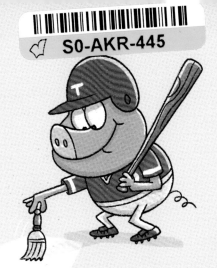

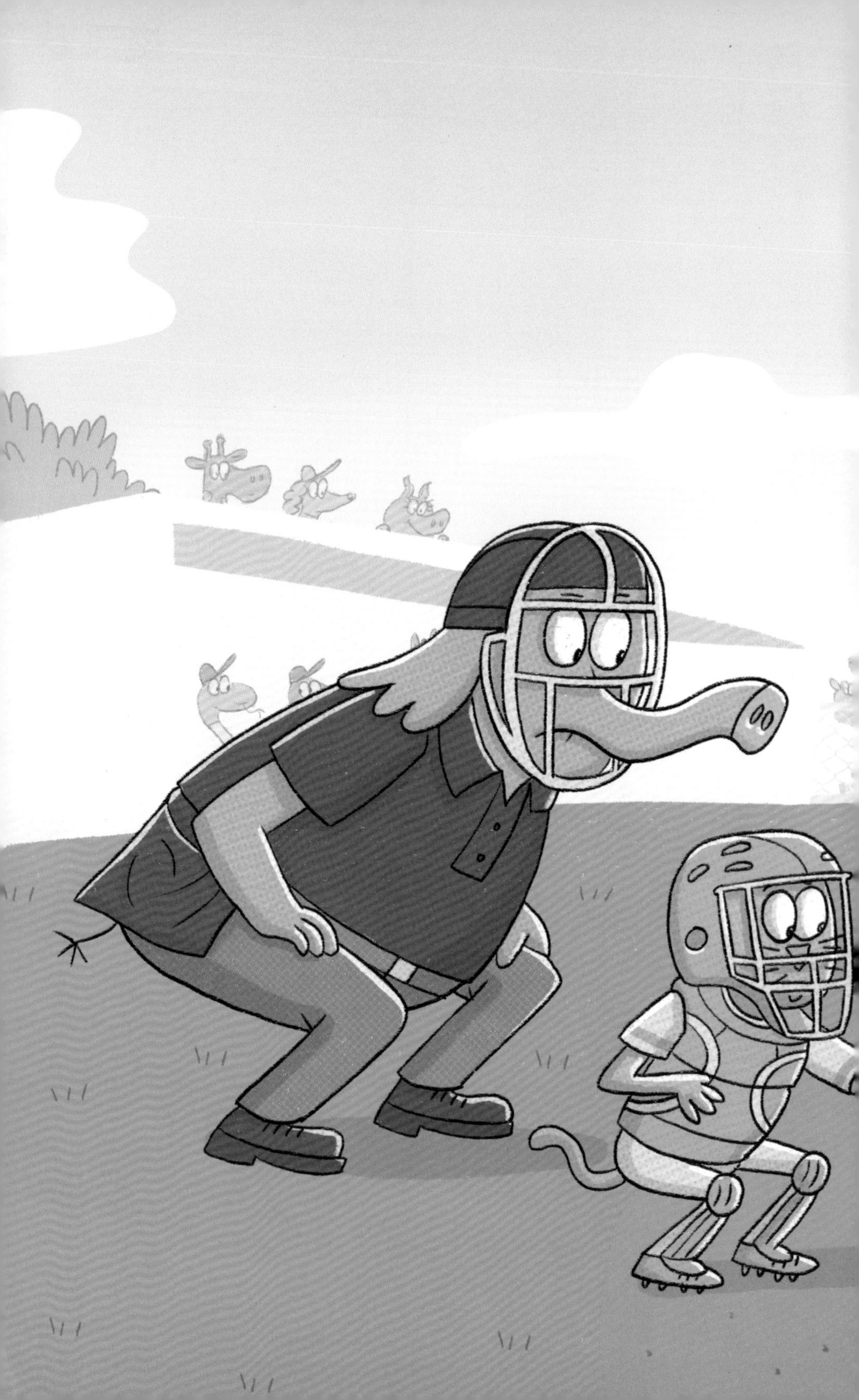

Ethan Long

HOGGY AT BAT

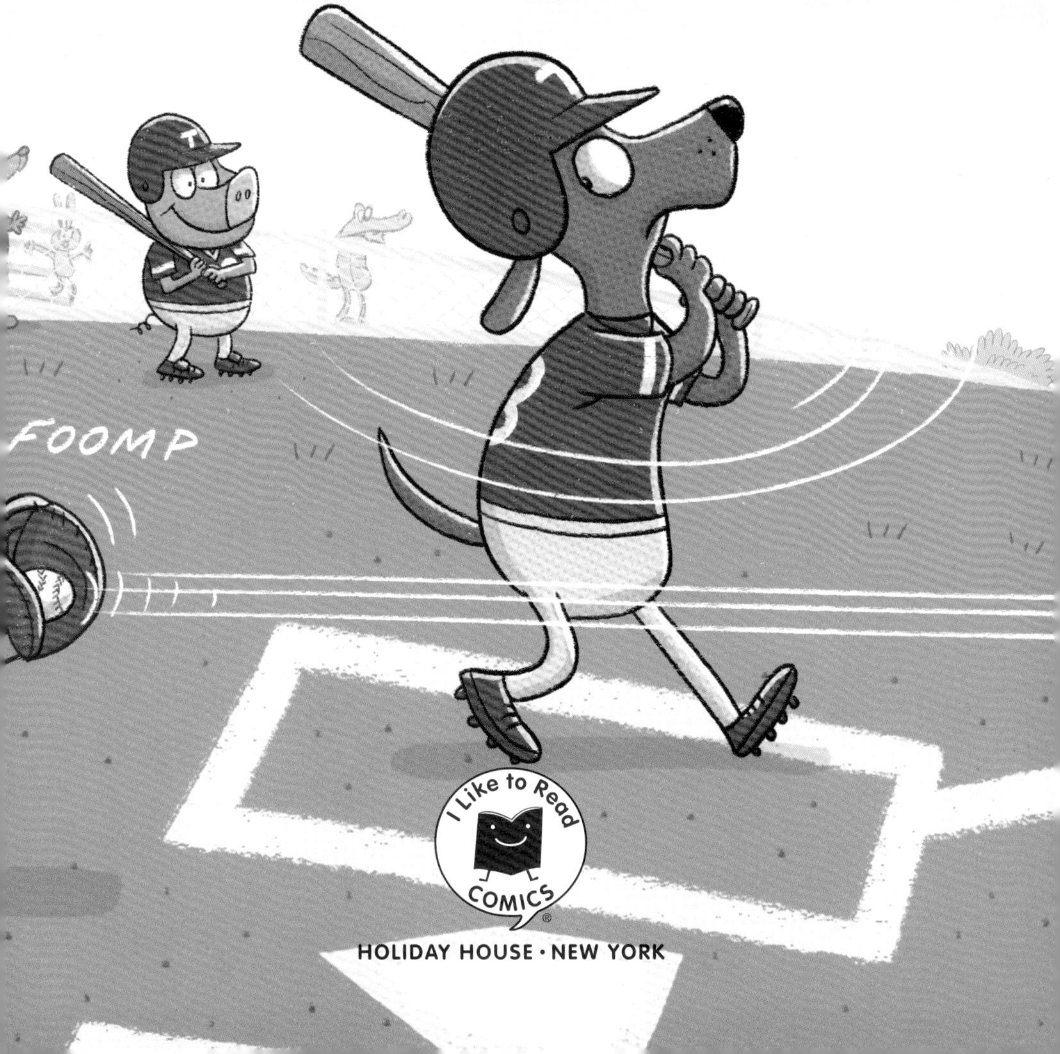
FOOMP

I Like to Read COMICS®

HOLIDAY HOUSE • NEW YORK

For Tug, Willie, and Alec

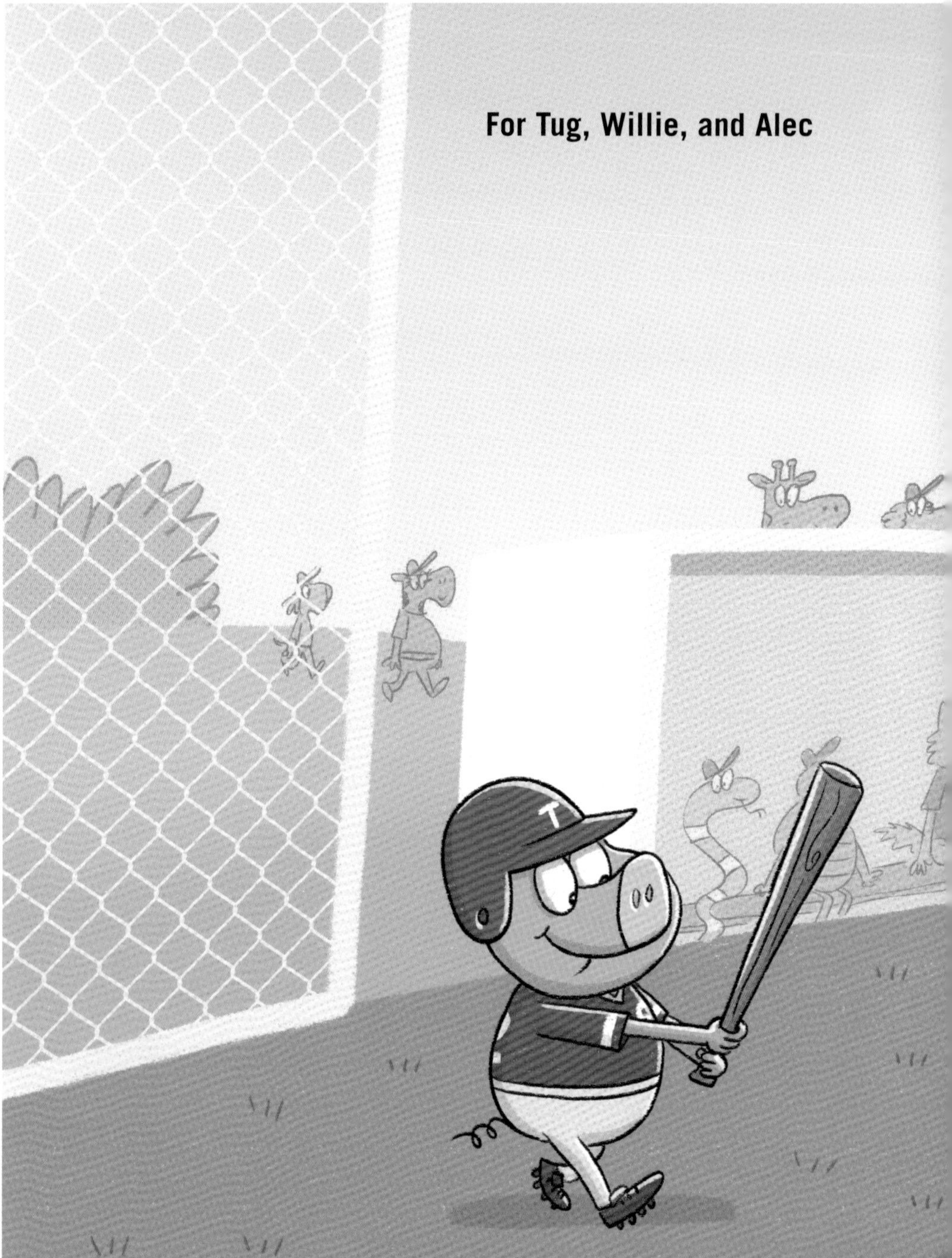

I Like to Read® Comics instill confidence and the joy of reading in new readers. Created by award-winning artists as well as talented newcomers, these imaginative books support beginners' reading comprehension with extensive visual support. We want to hear every new reader say, "I like to read comics!"

Visit our website for flash cards, activities, and more about the series:
www.holidayhouse.com/ILiketoRead
#ILTR

Printed and bound in July 2023 at C&C Offset, Shenzhen, China.
The artwork was created digitally. www.holidayhouse.com
First Edition
1 3 5 7 9 10 8 6 4 2

Library of Congress Cataloging-in-Publication Data is available.
ISBN 978-0-8234-5149-4 (hardcover)

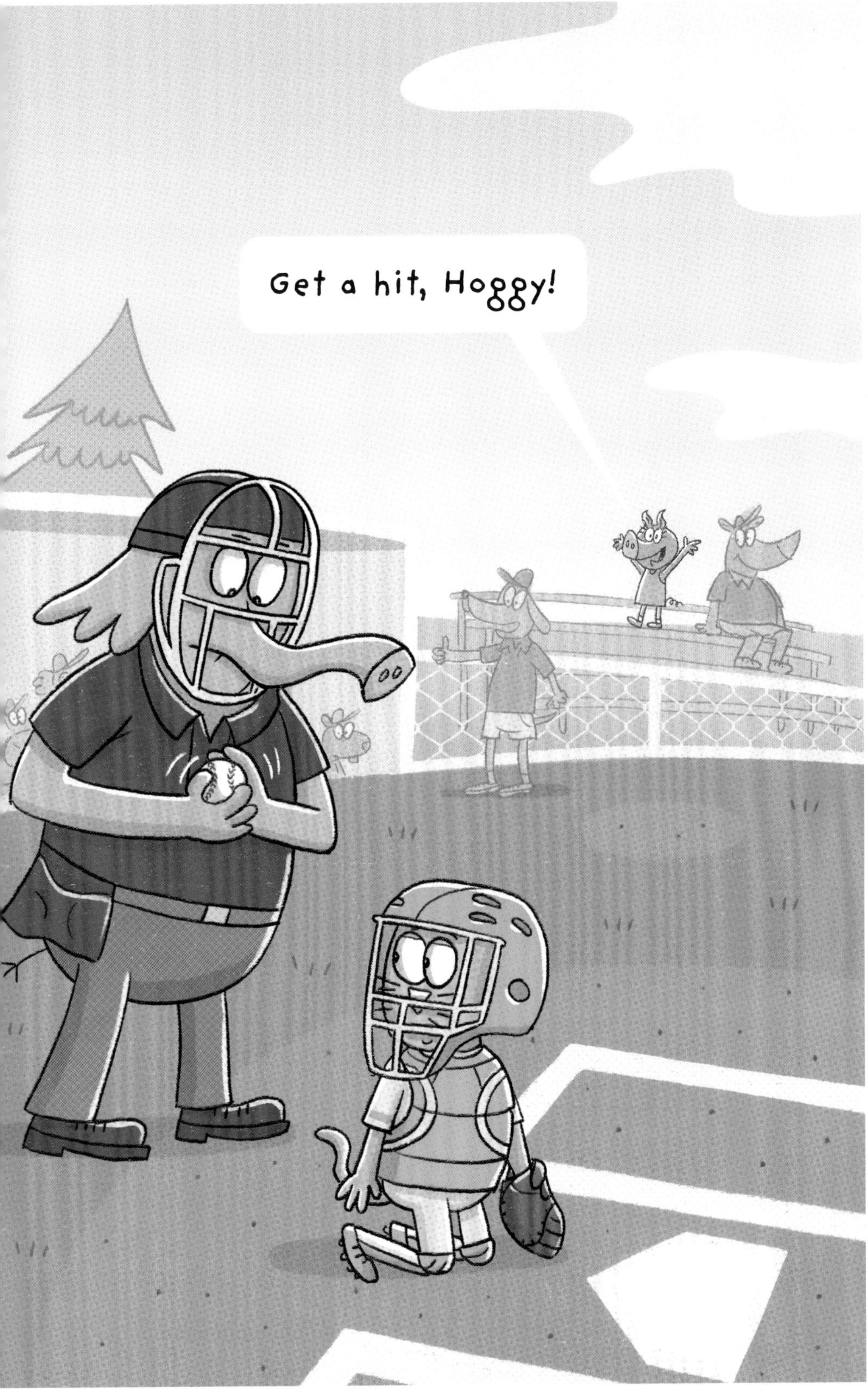
Get a hit, Hoggy!

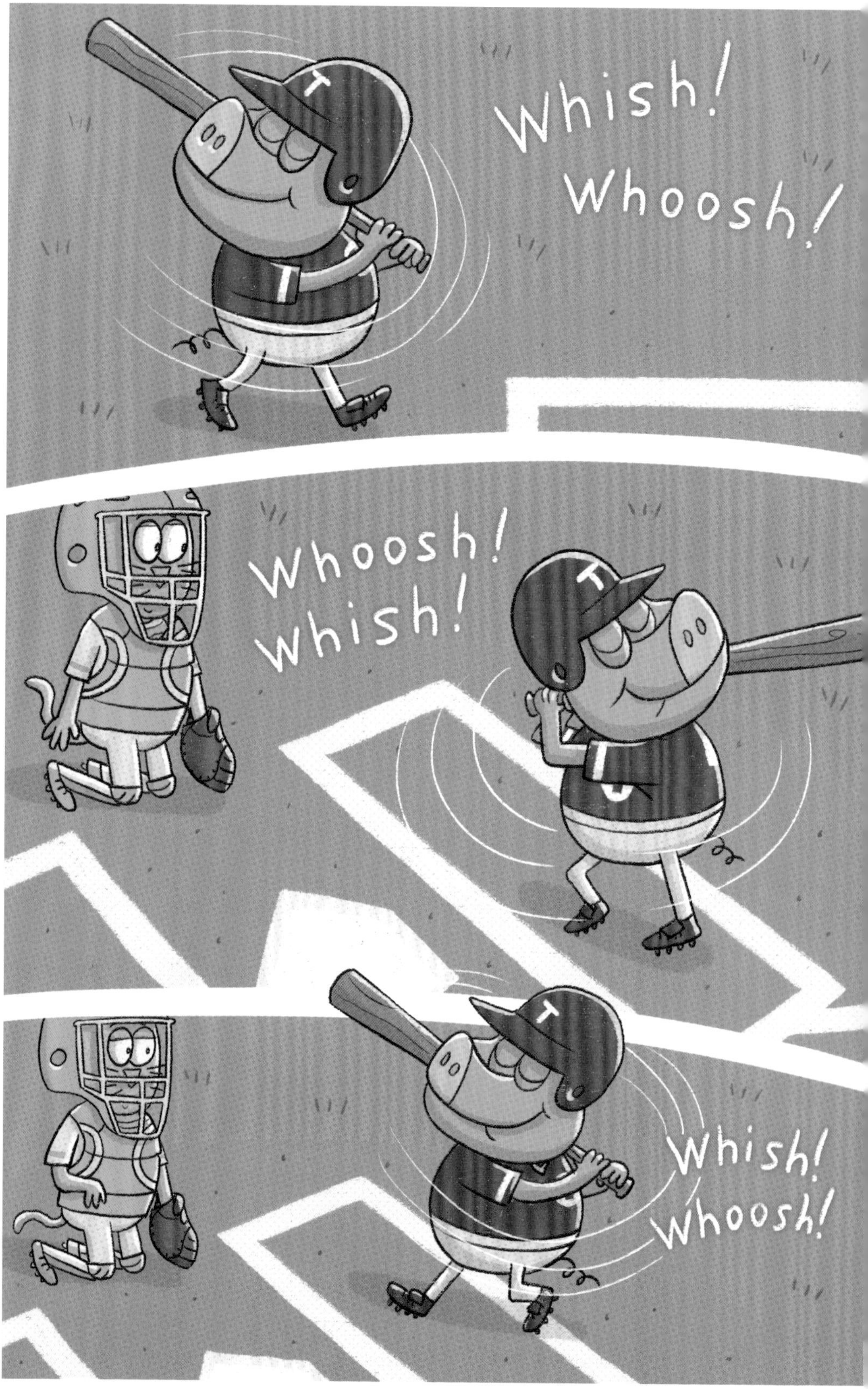
Whish!
Whoosh!
Whoosh!
Whish!
Whish!
Whoosh!

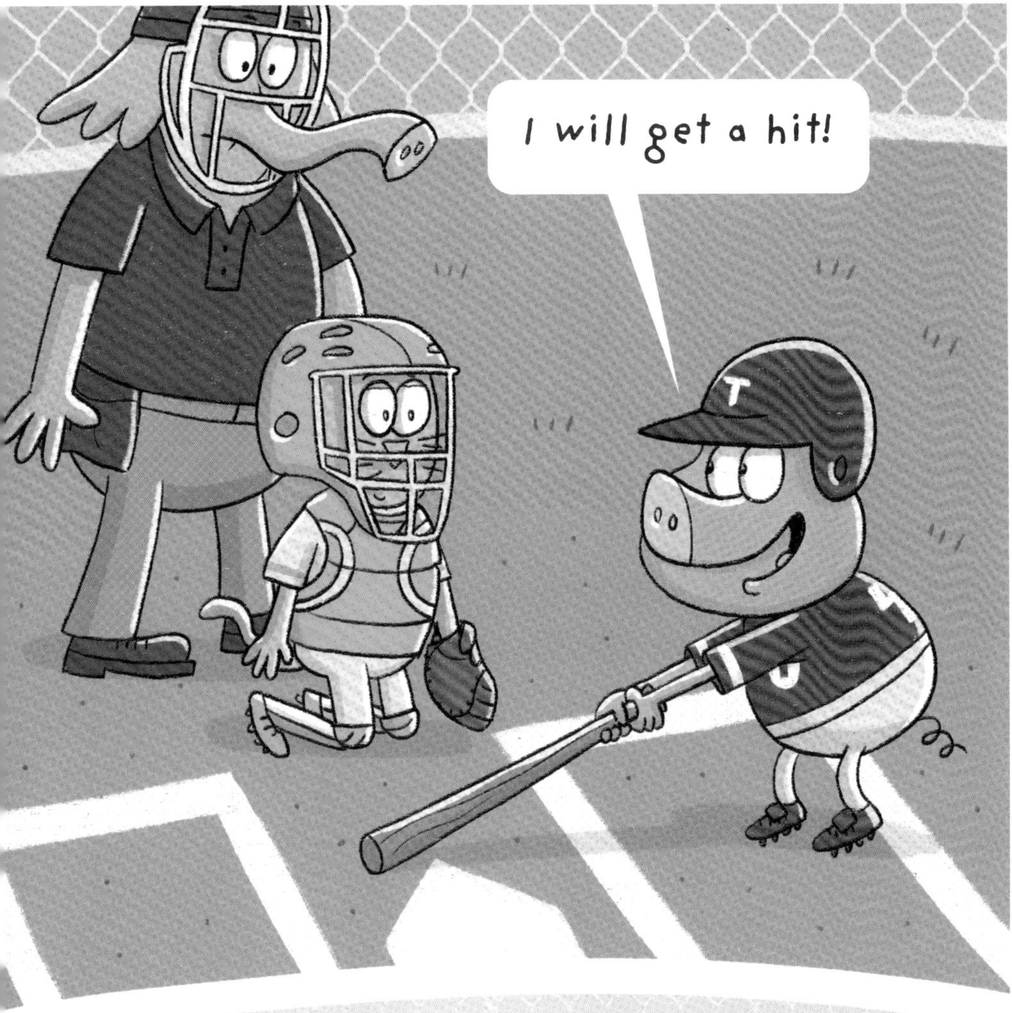
I will get a hit!

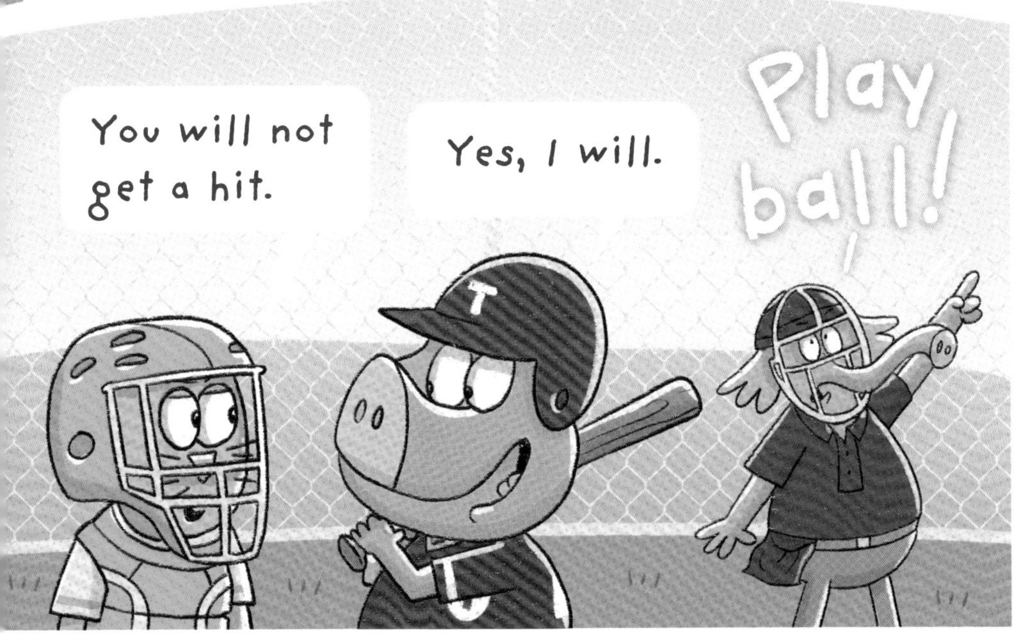
You will not get a hit.
Yes, I will.
Play ball!

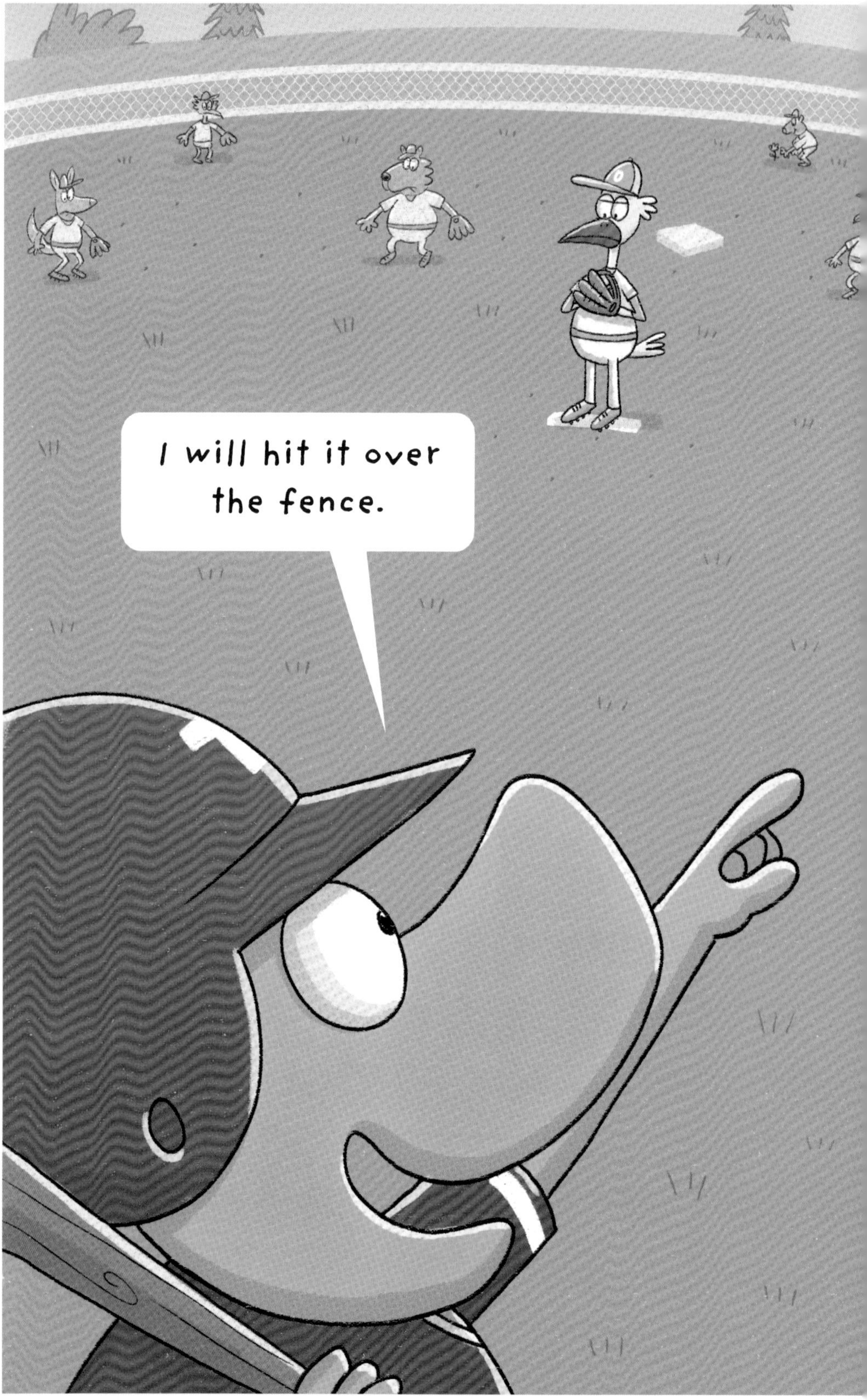
I will hit it over the fence.

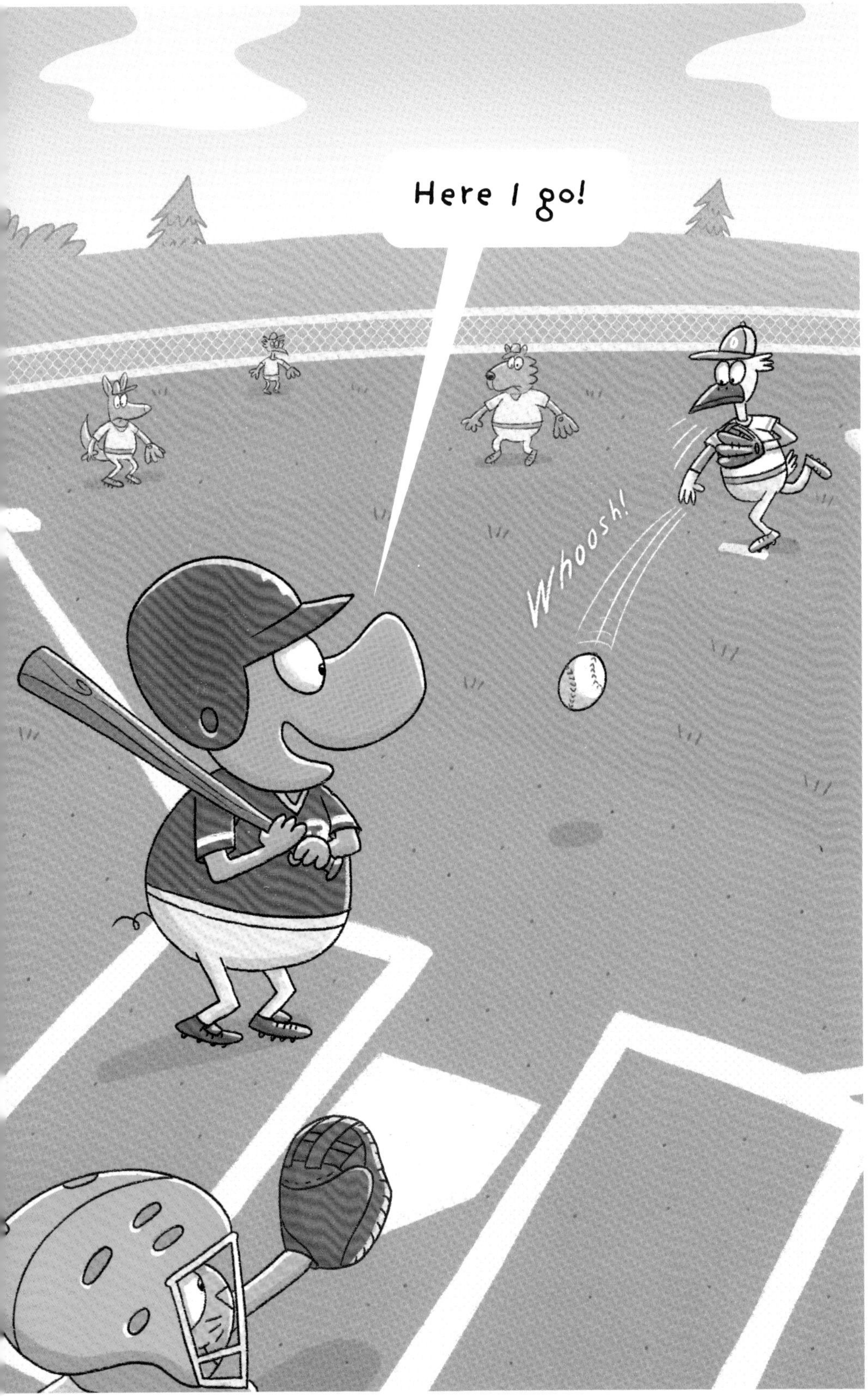
Here I go!
Whoosh!

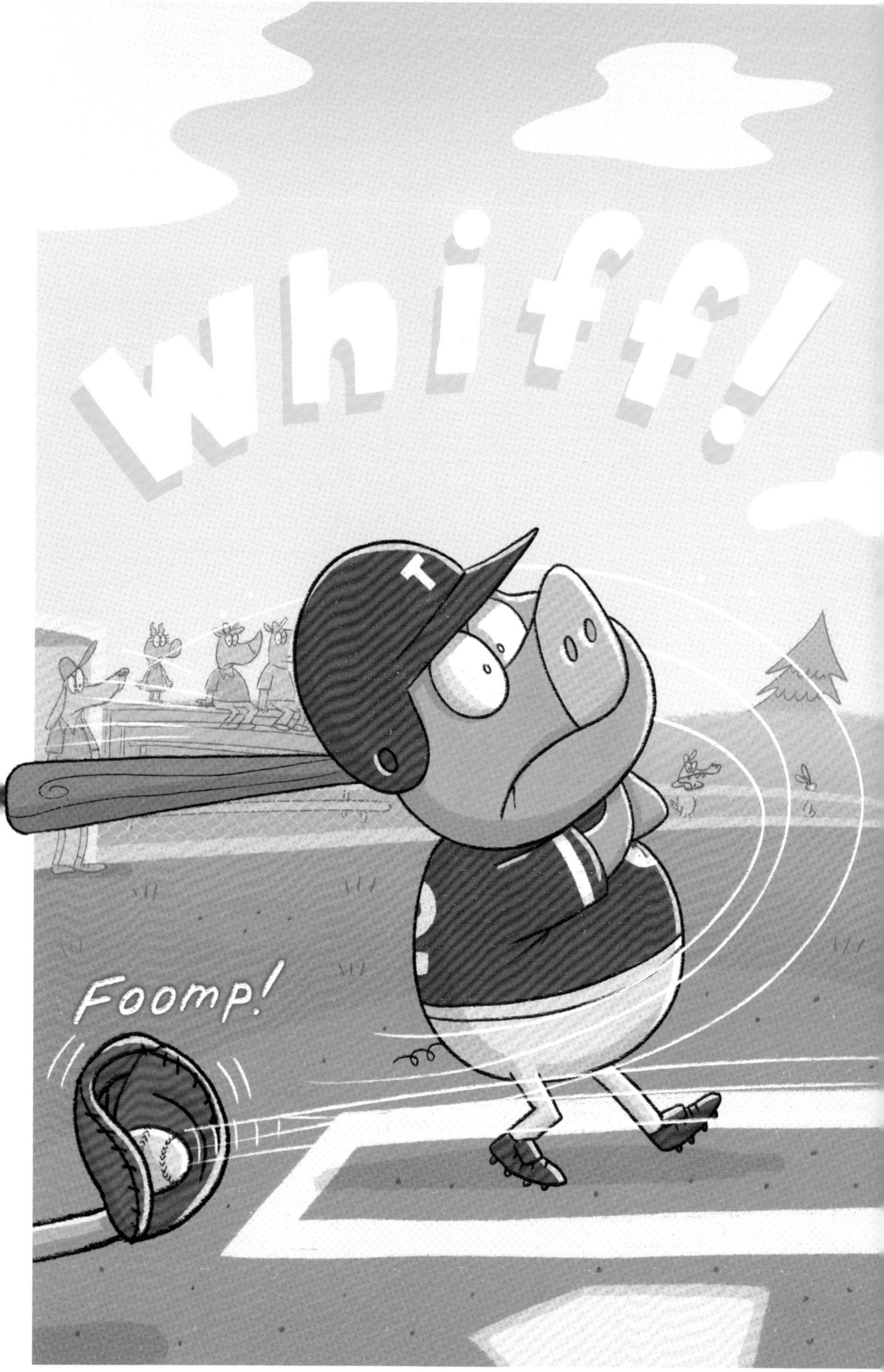
Whiff!
Foomp!

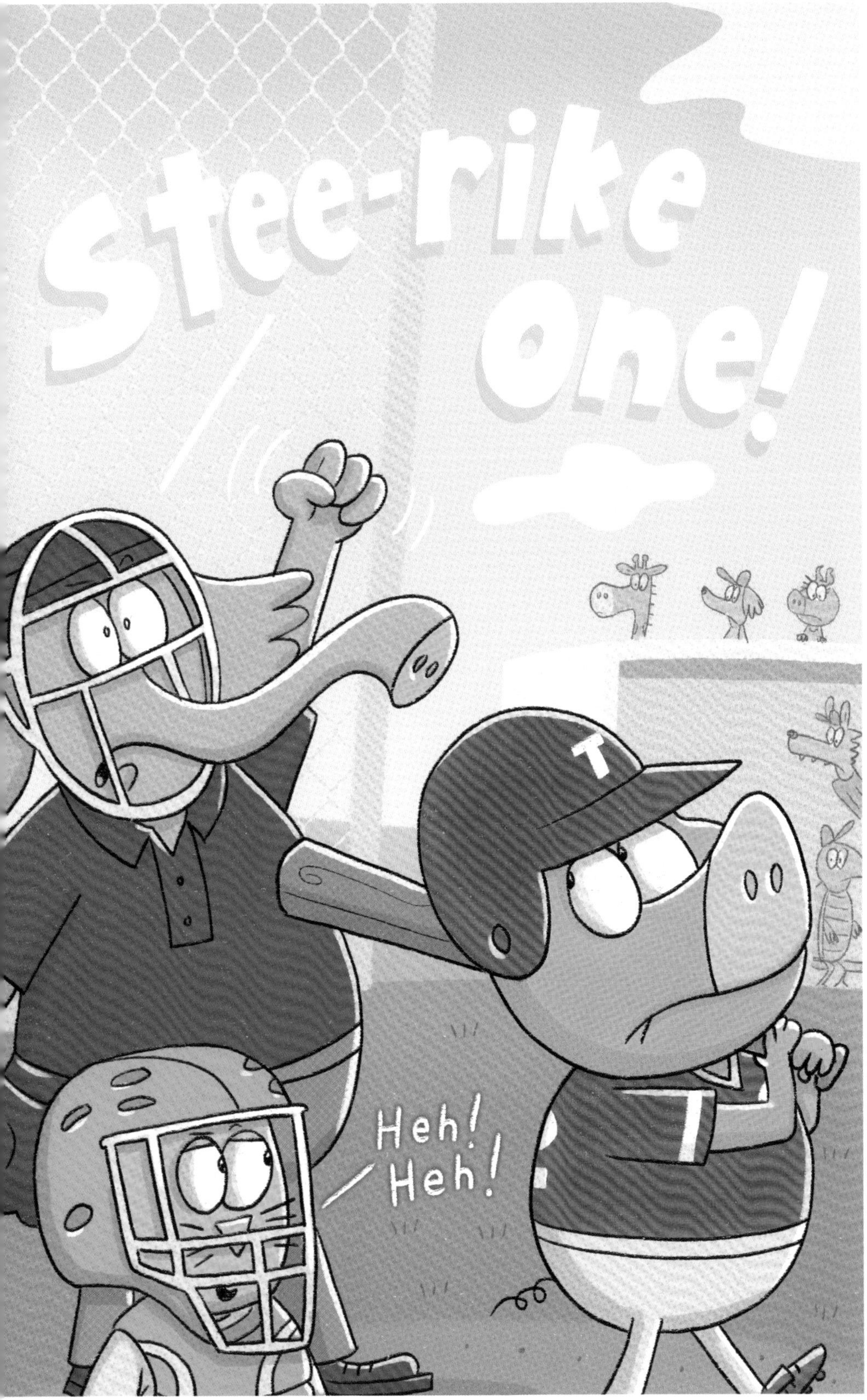
Stee-rike One!
Heh! Heh!

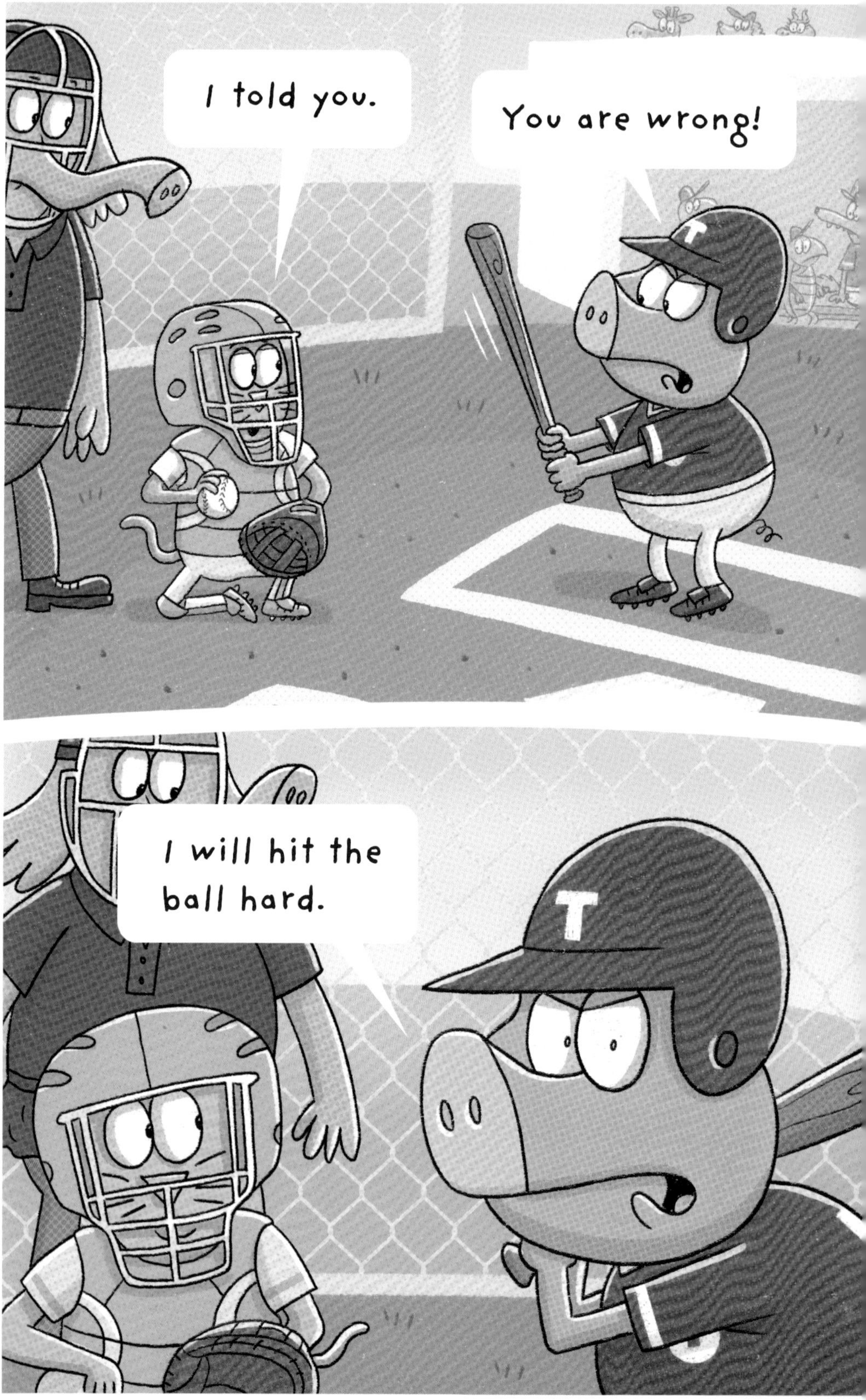
I told you.
You are wrong!
I will hit the ball hard.

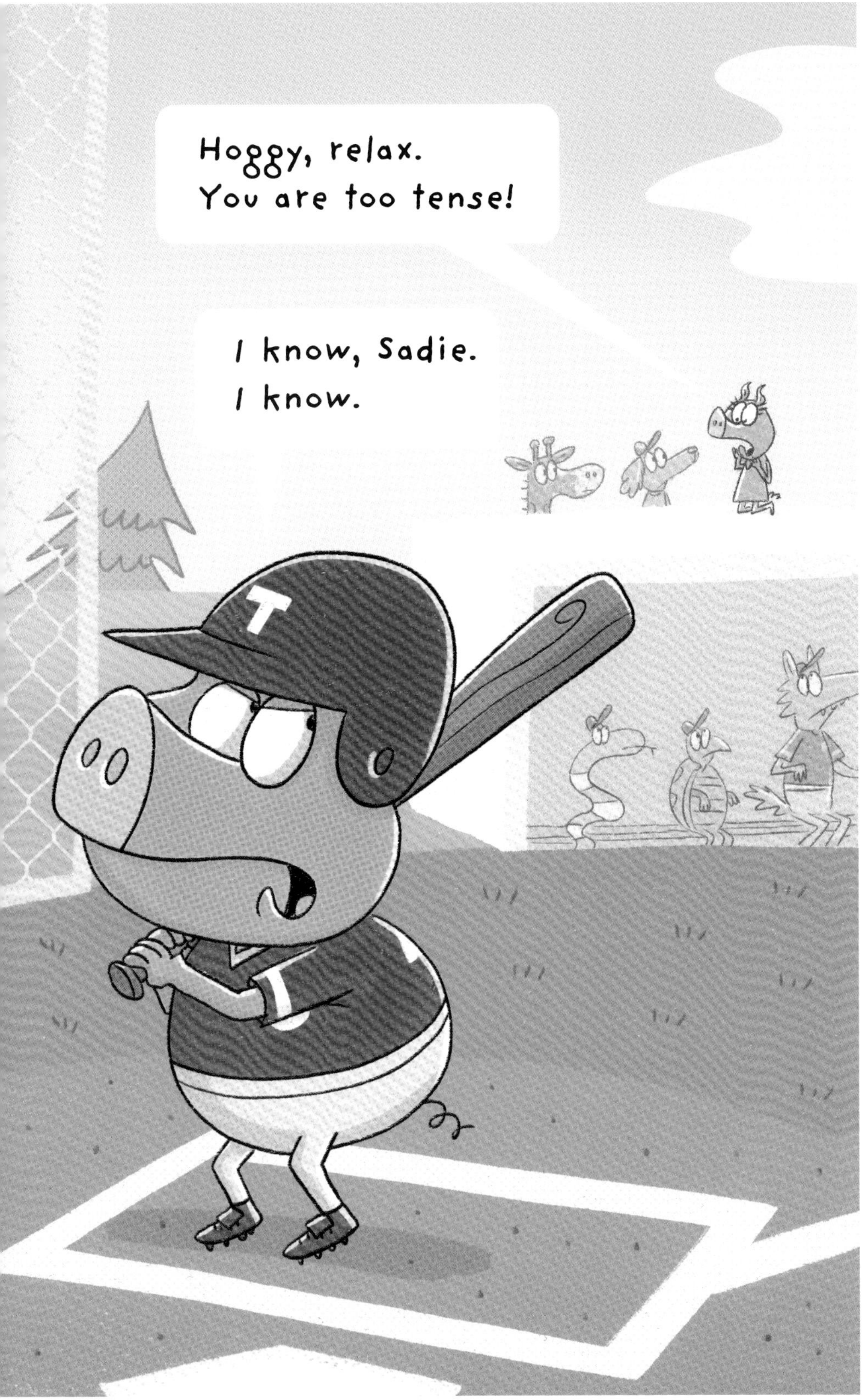
Hoggy, relax. You are too tense!
I know, Sadie. I know.

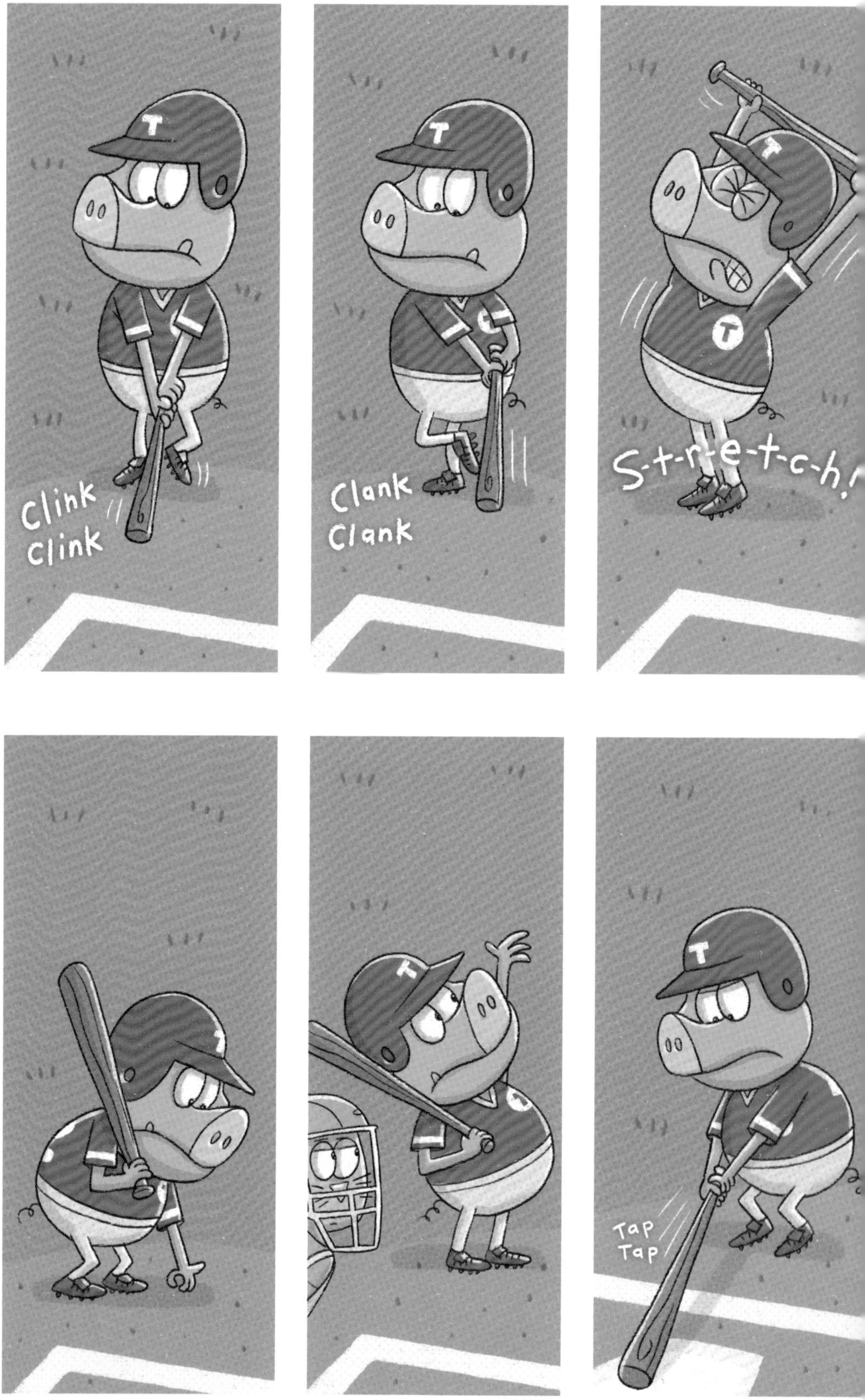
Clink
Clink
Clank
Clank
S-t-r-e-t-c-h!
Tap
Tap

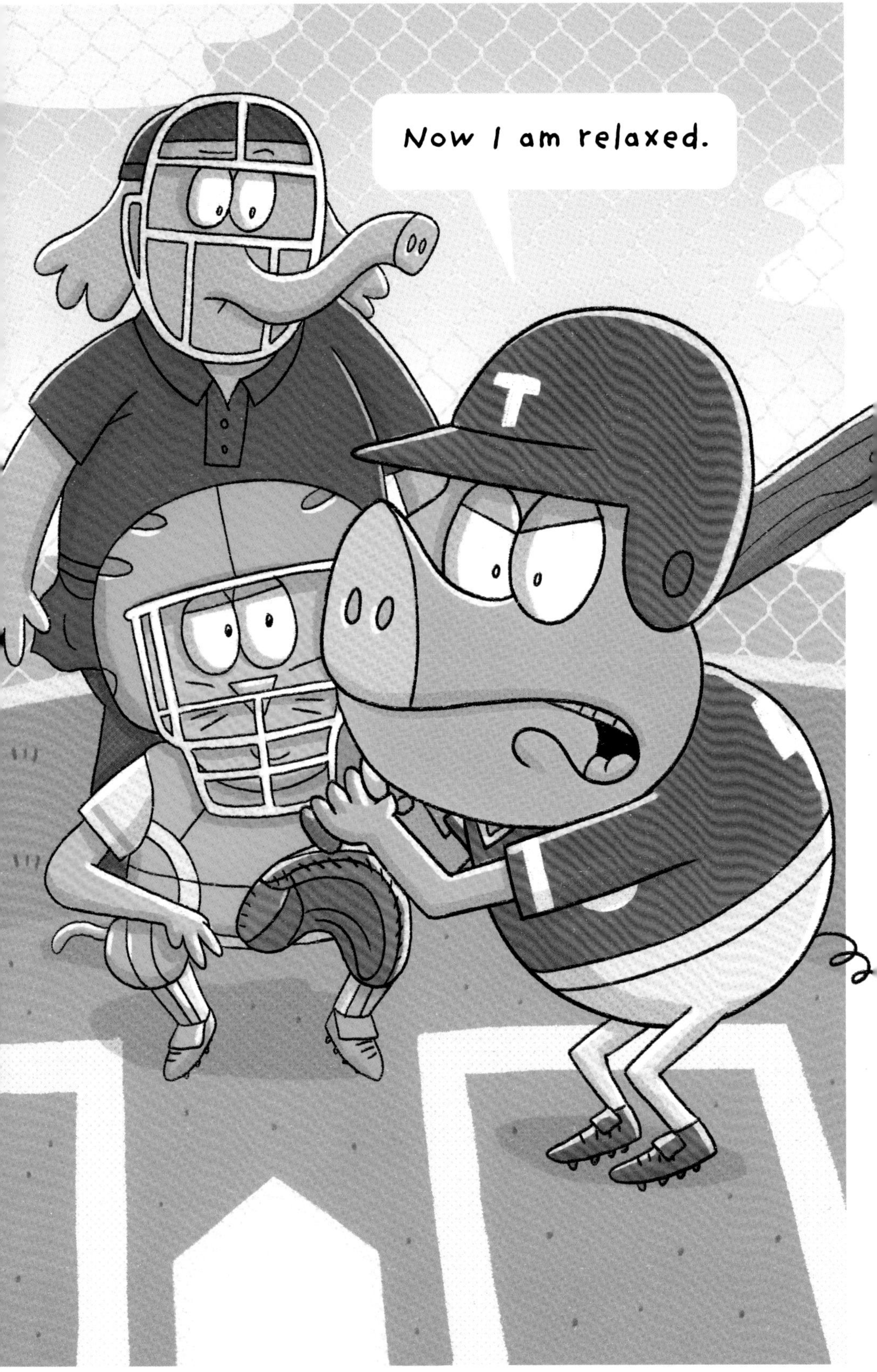
Now I am relaxed.

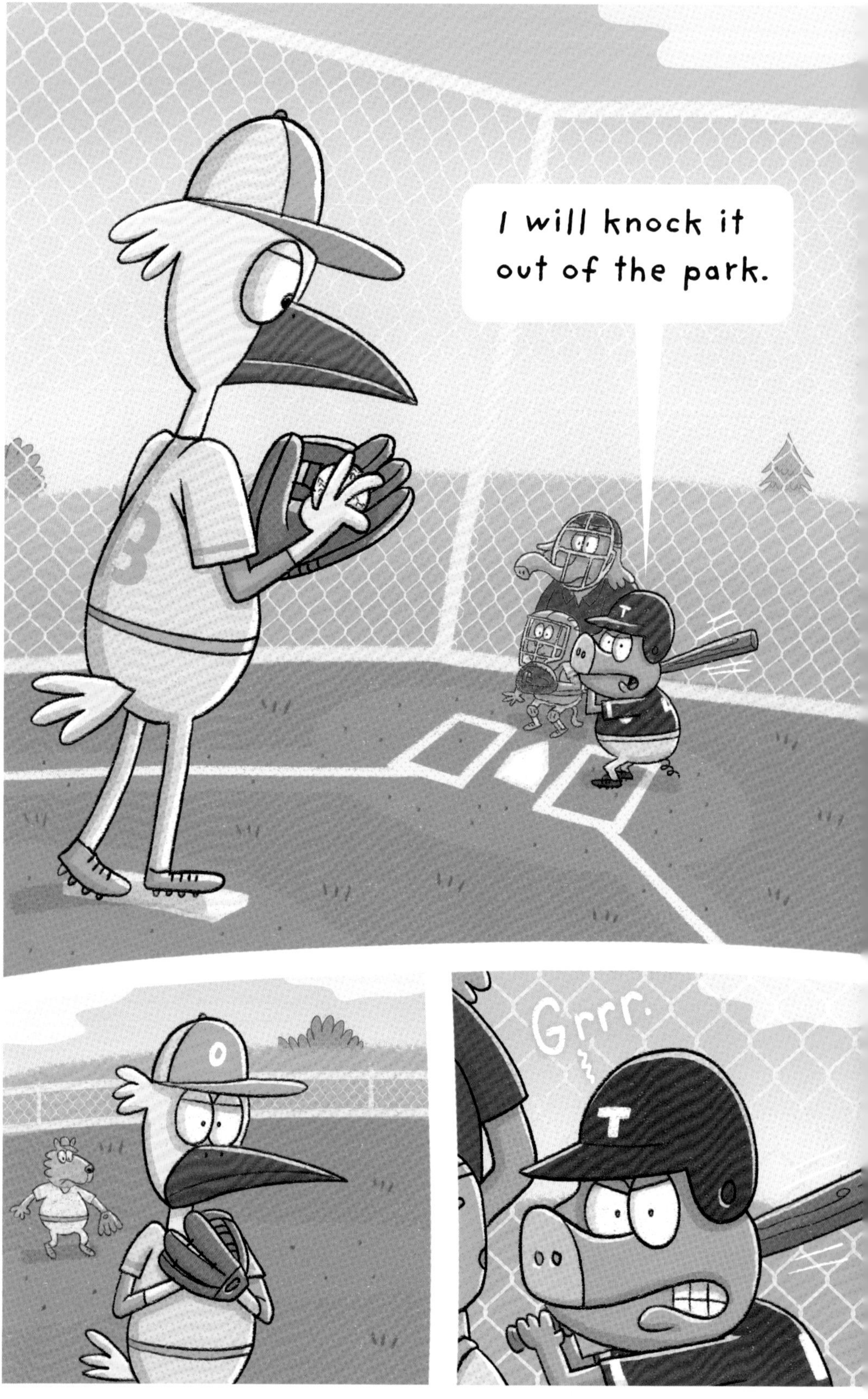
I will knock it out of the park.
Grrr.

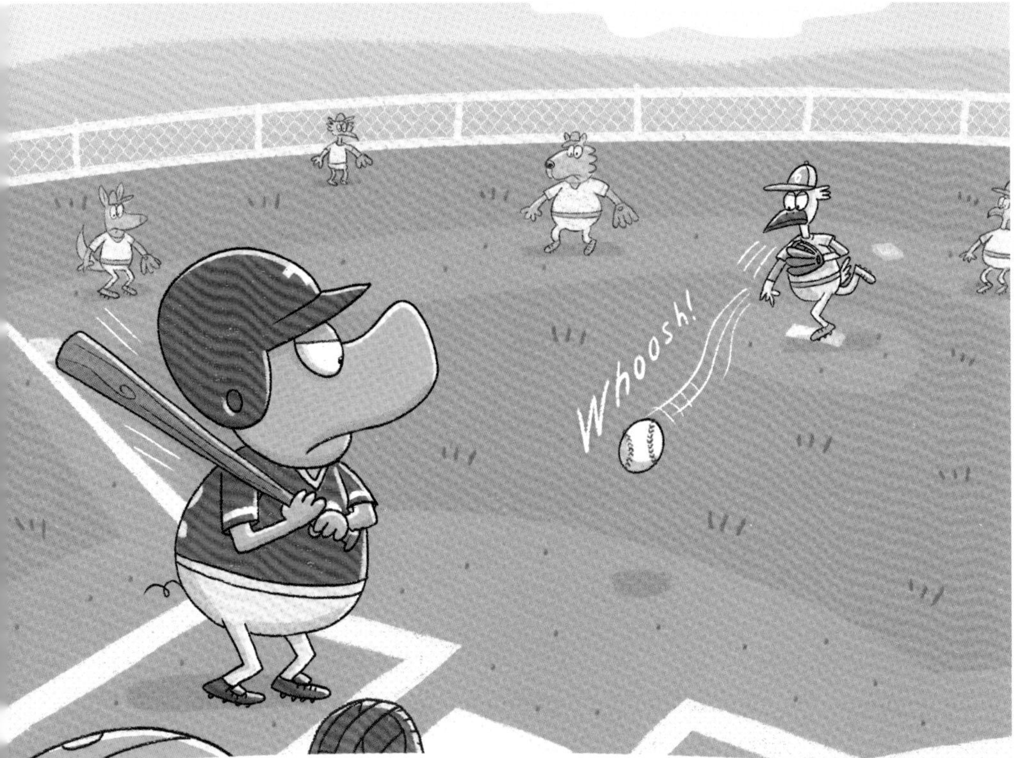
Whoosh!

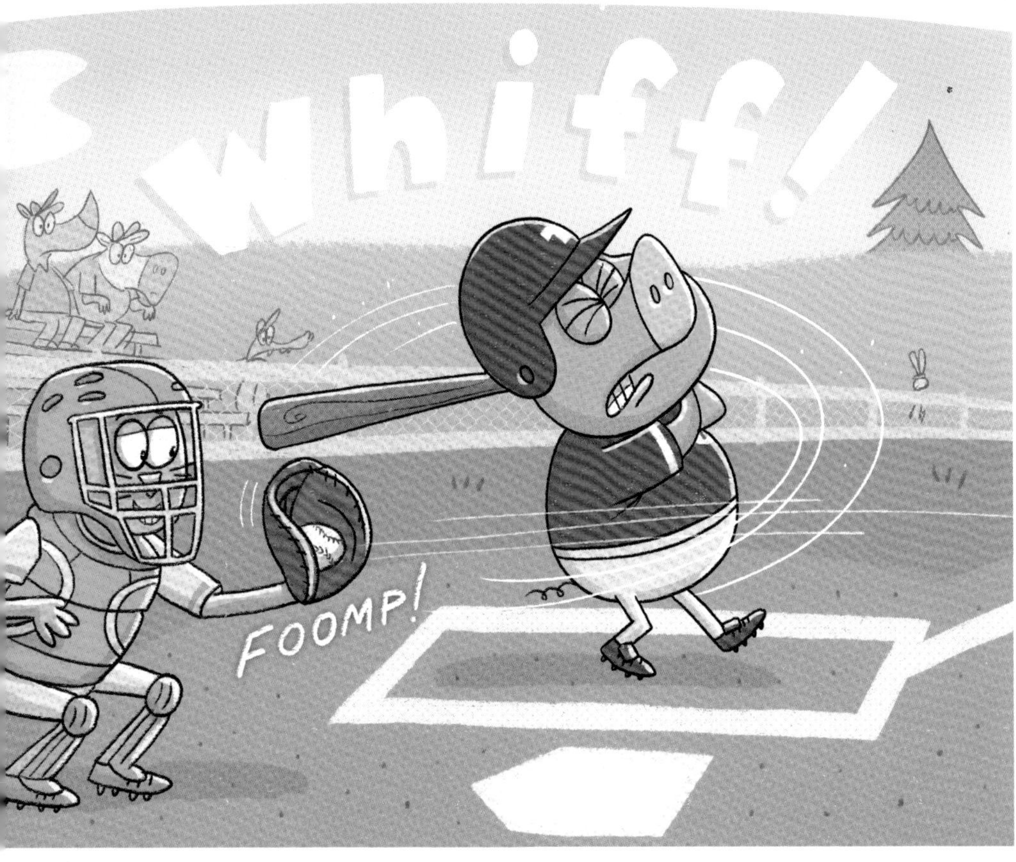
Whiff!
FOOMP!

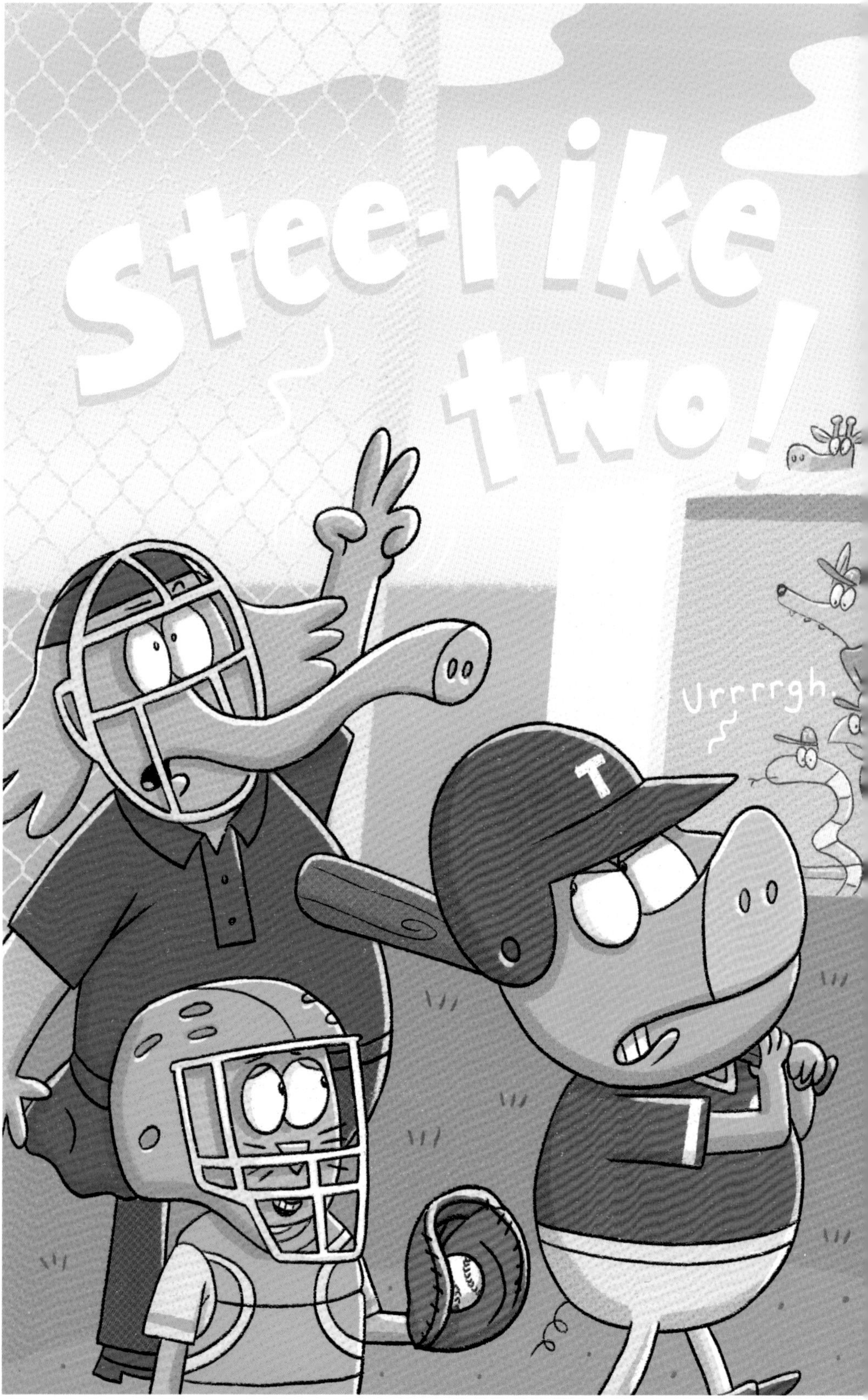
Stee-rike two!
Urrrrgh.

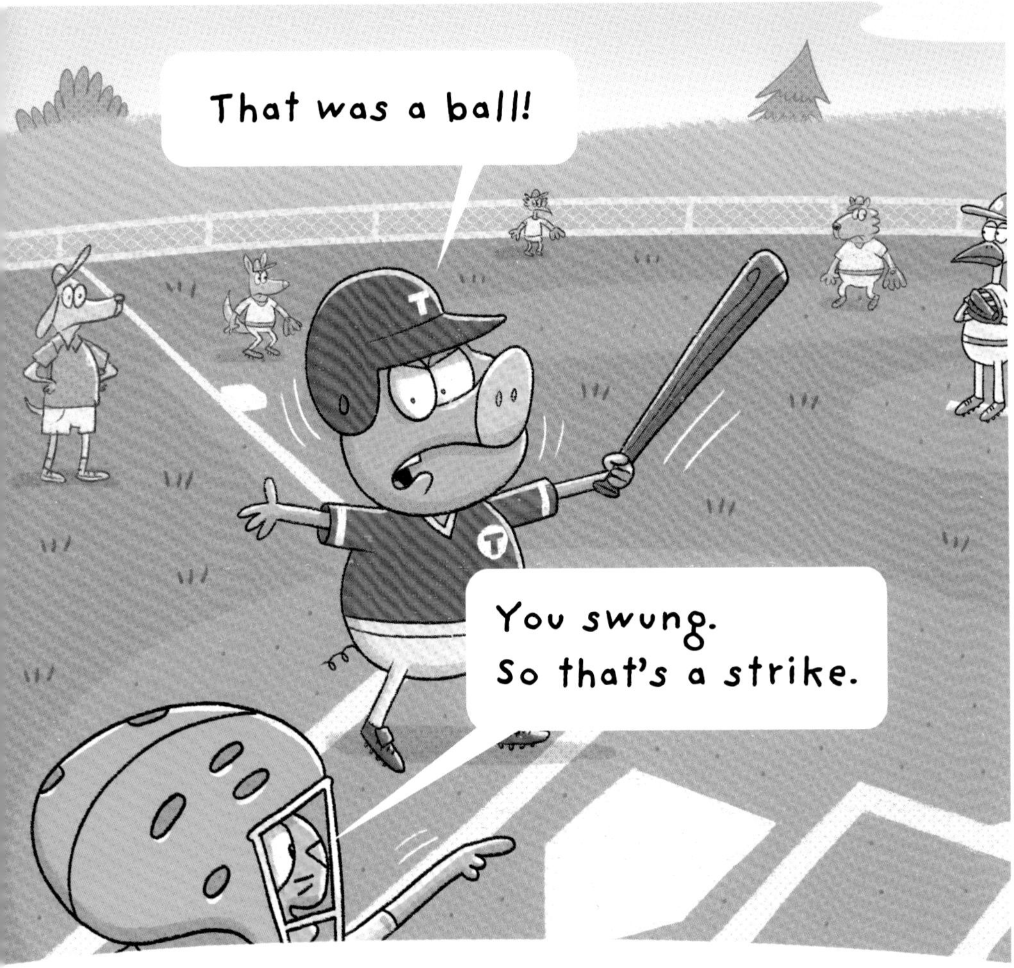
That was a ball!
You swung.
So that's a strike.

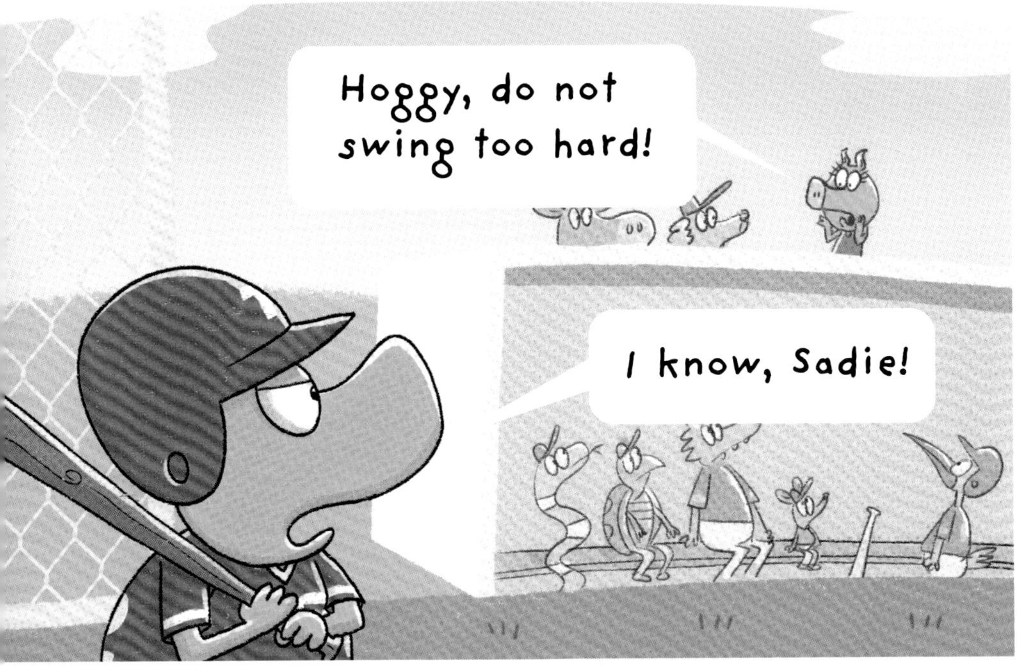
Hoggy, do not
swing too hard!
I know, Sadie!

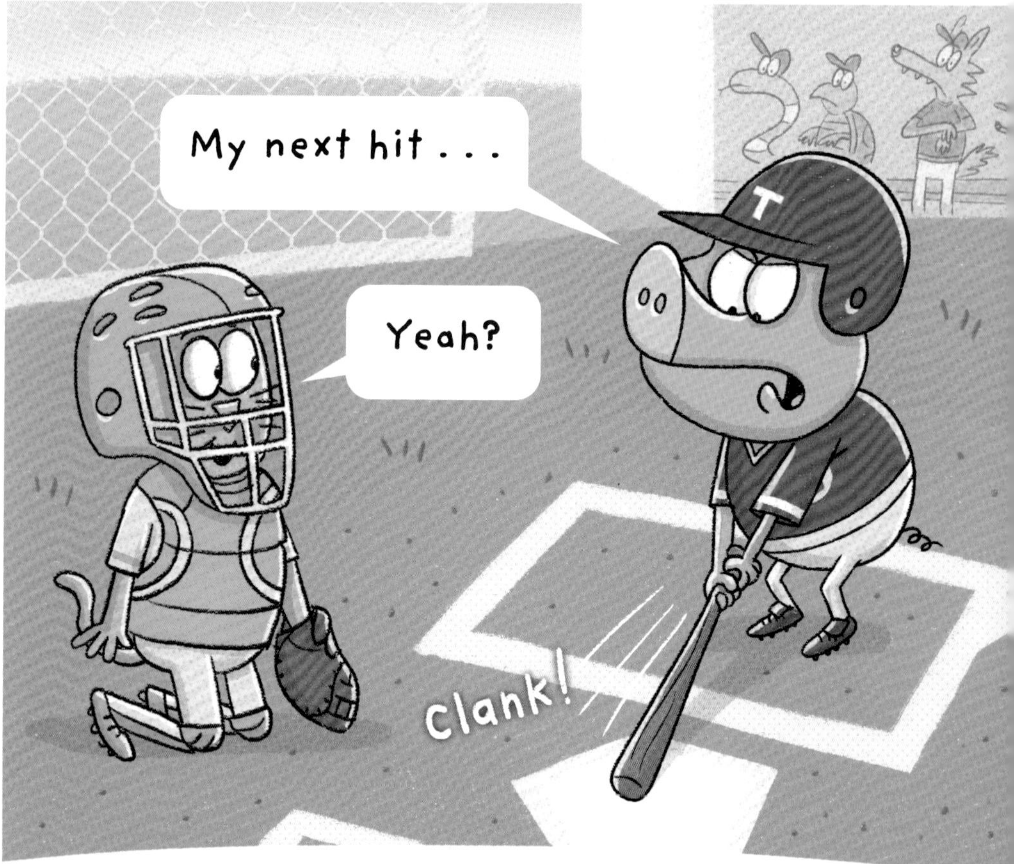
My next hit . . .
Yeah?
Clank!

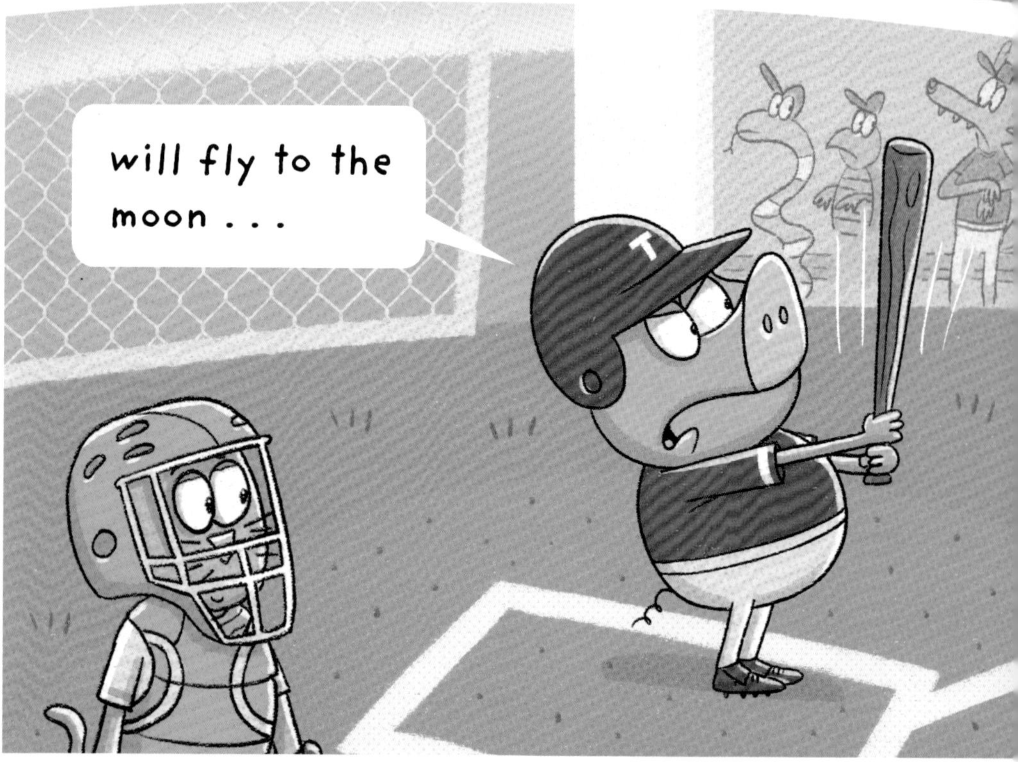
will fly to the moon . . .

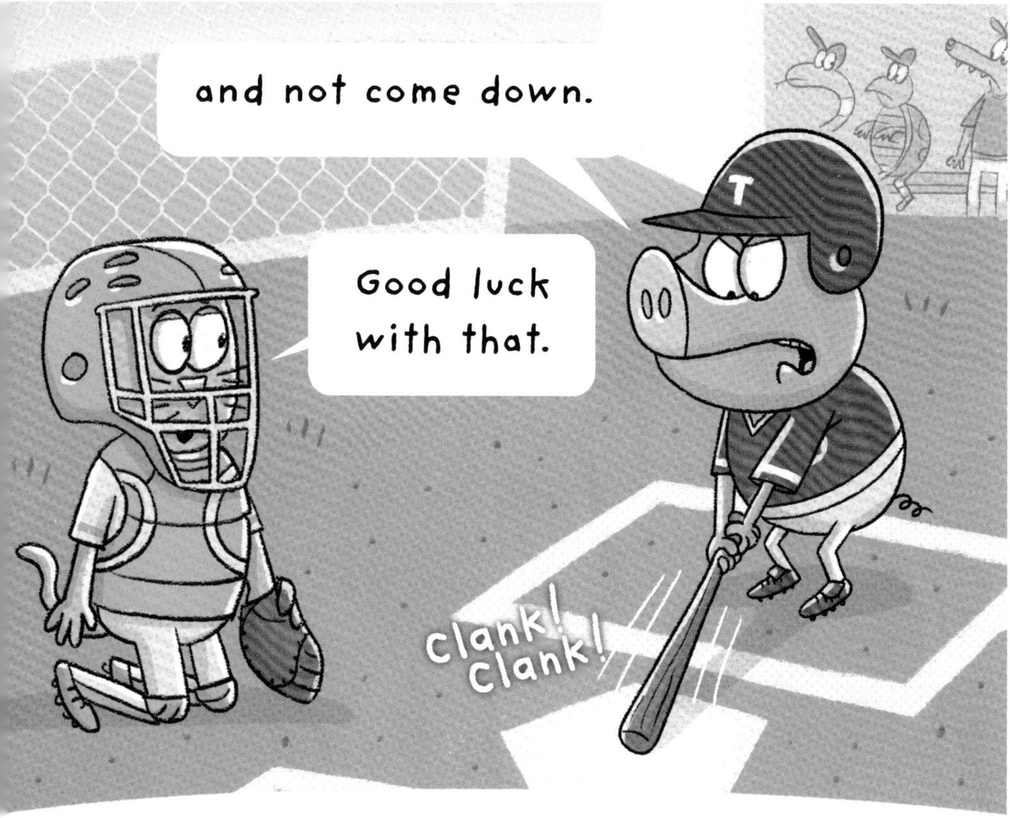
and not come down.
Good luck with that.
Clank! Clank!

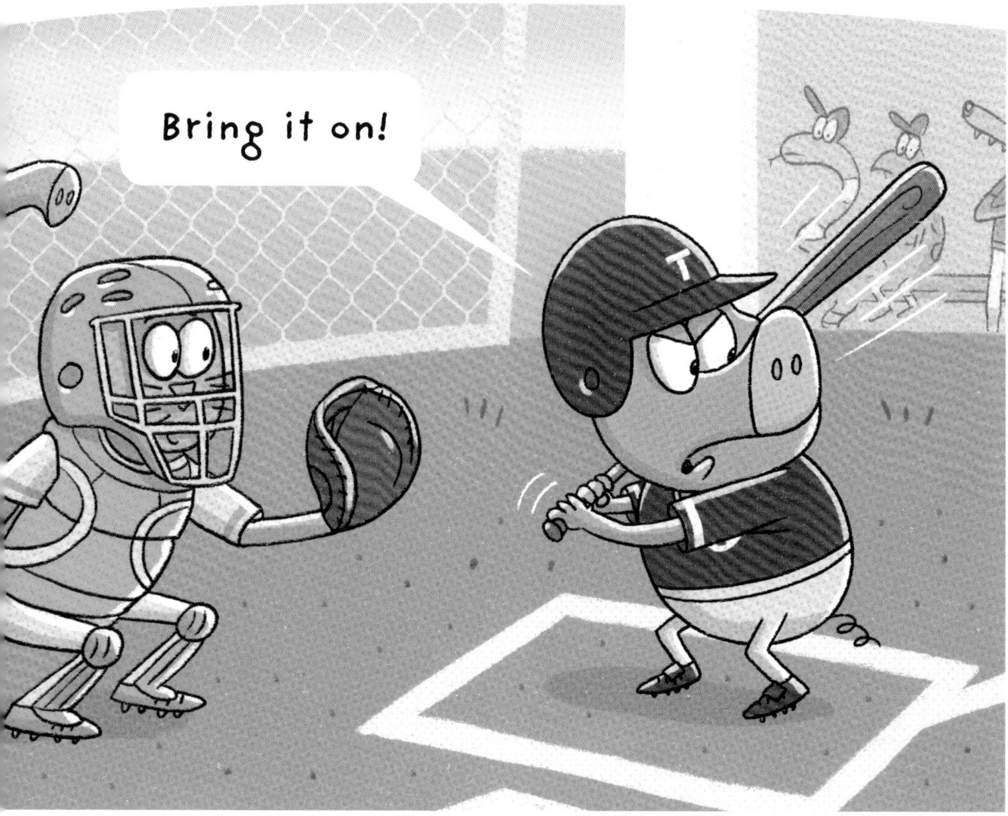
Bring it on!

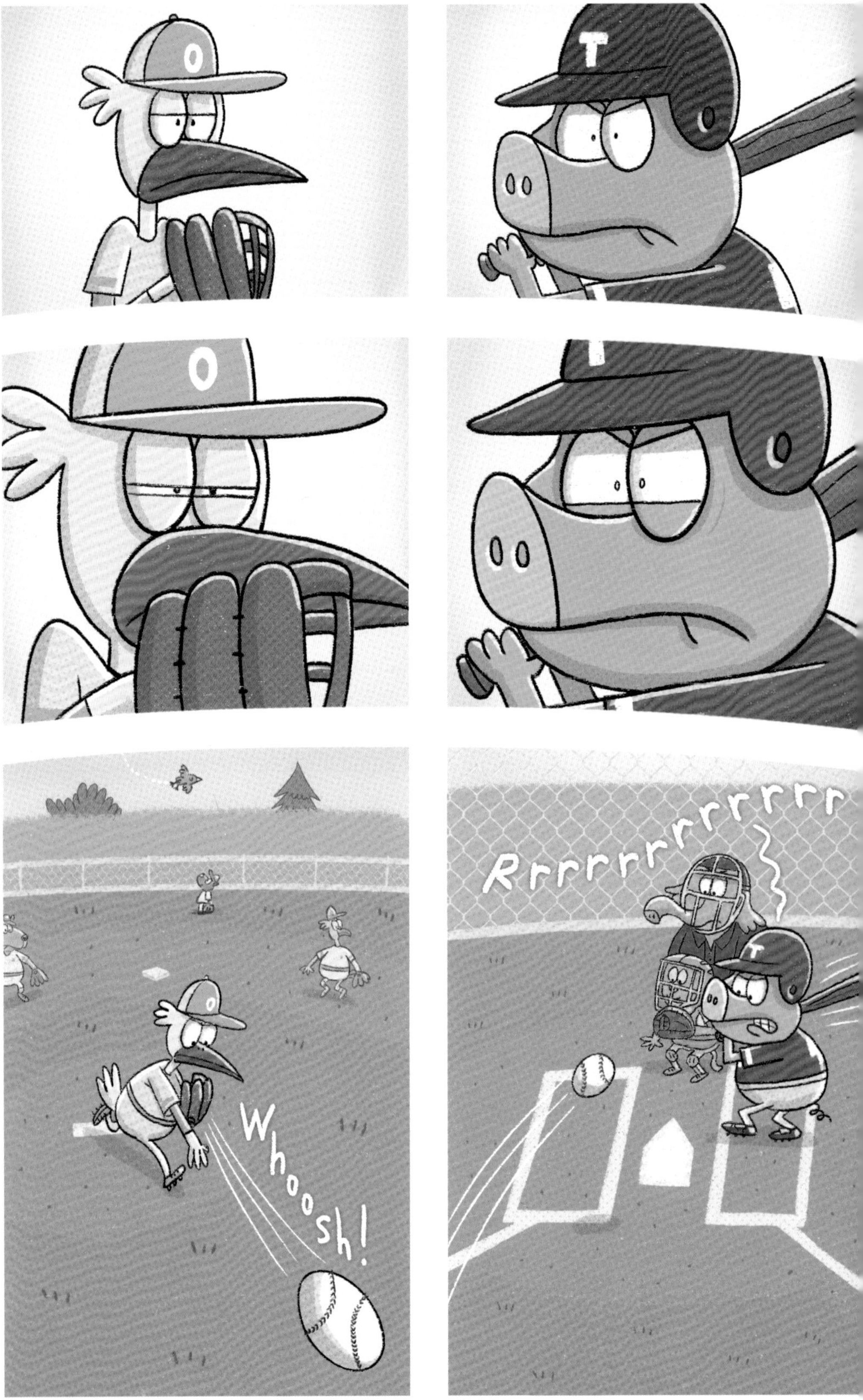
Whooosh!
Rrrrrrrrrrrrrr

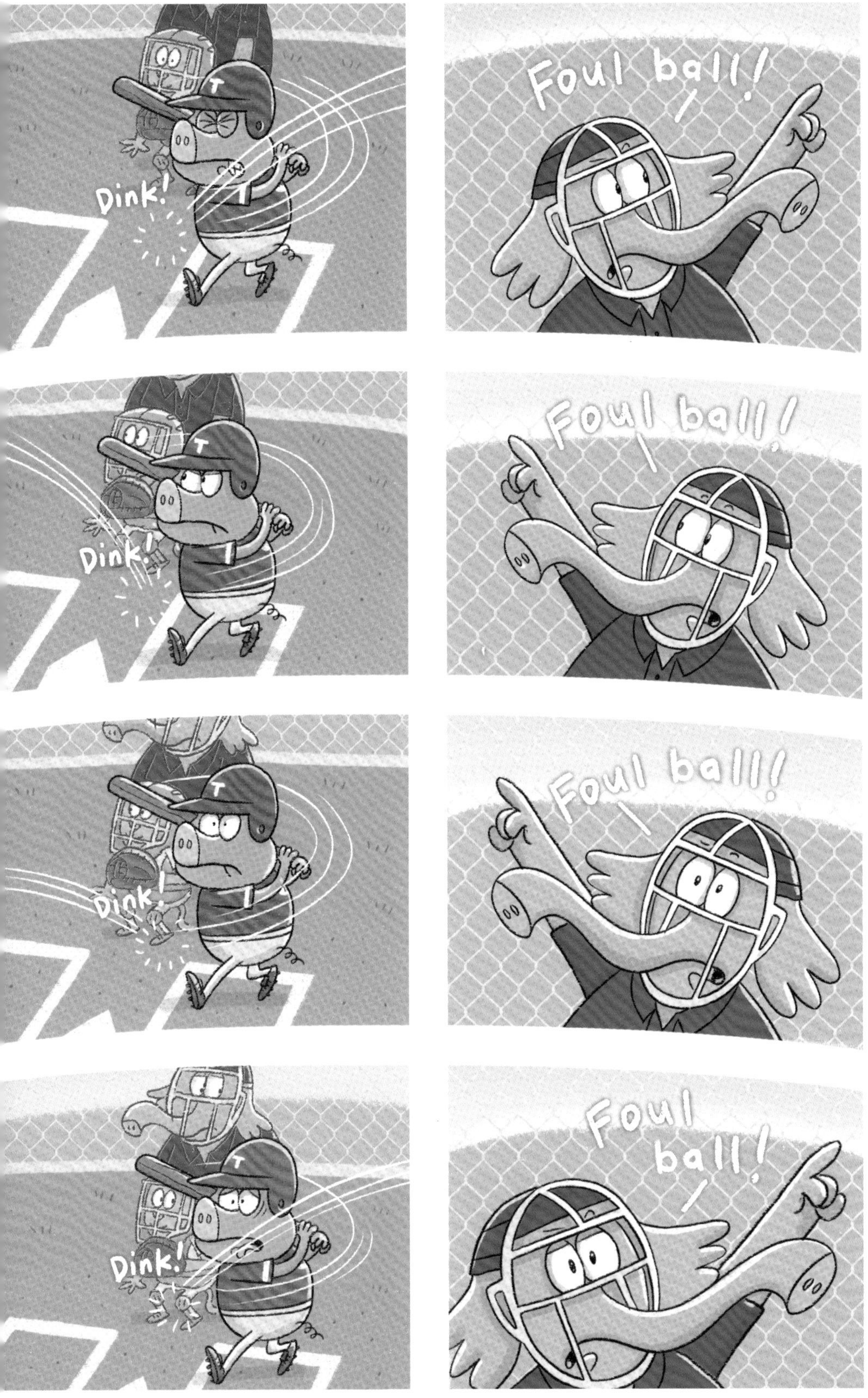
Dink!
Foul ball!
Dink!
Foul ball!
Dink!
Foul ball!
Dink!
Foul
ball!

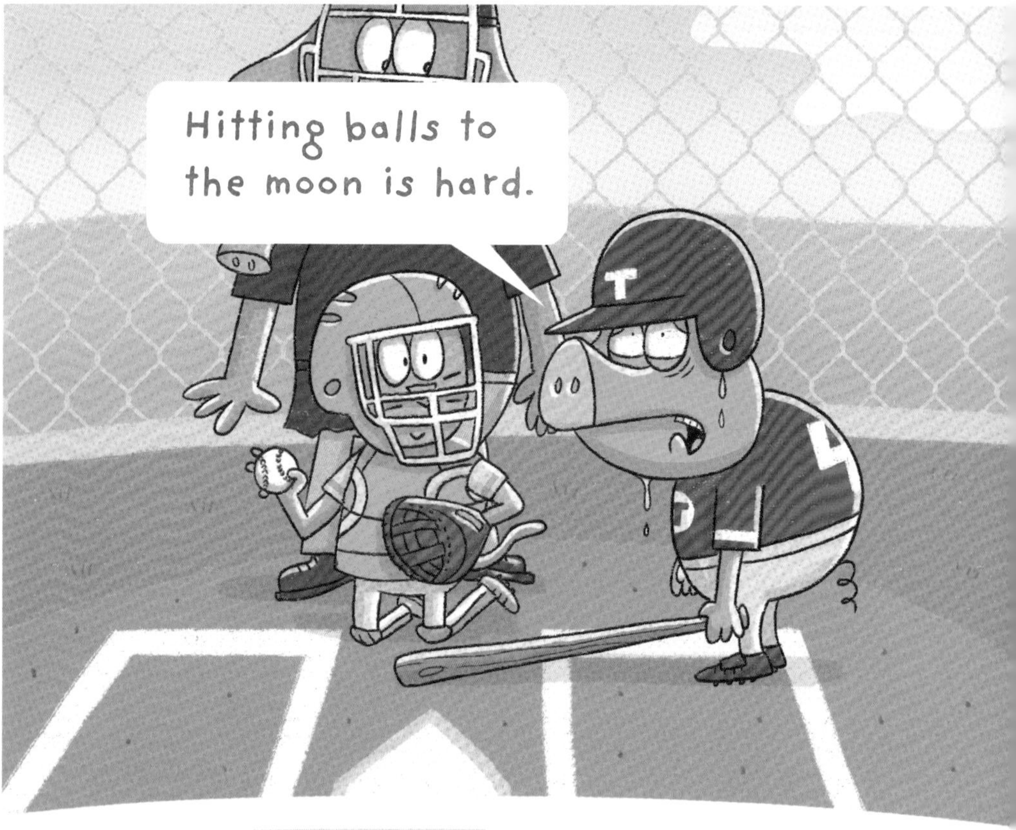
Hitting balls to
the moon is hard.

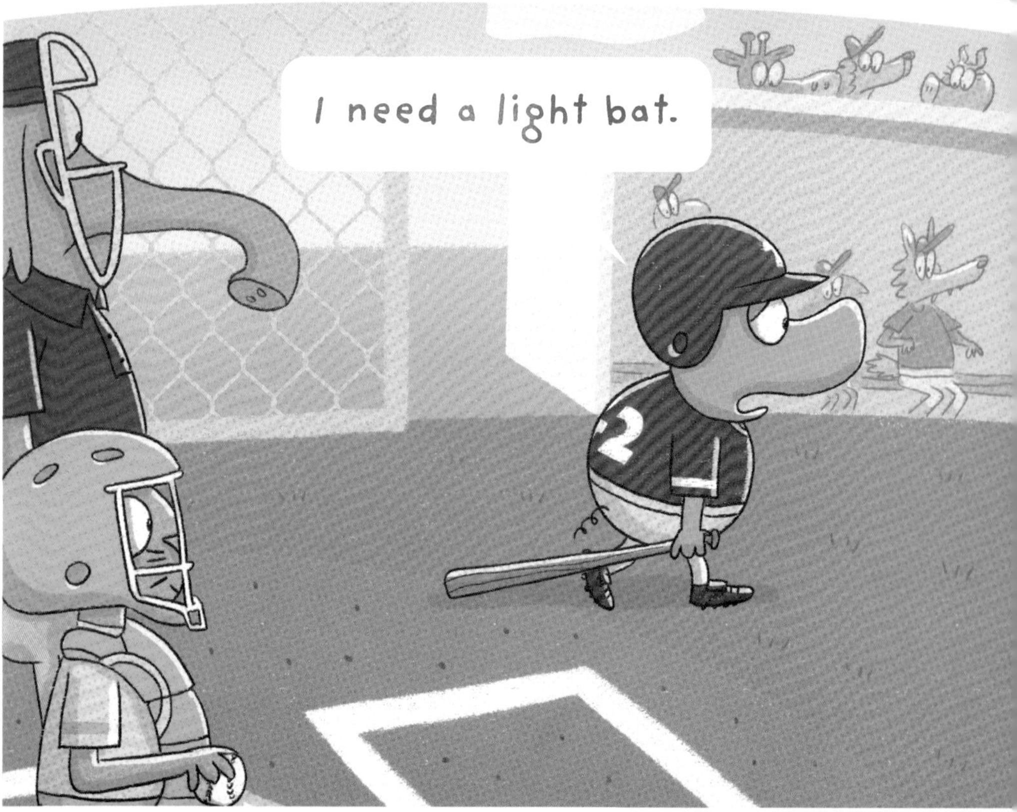
I need a light bat.

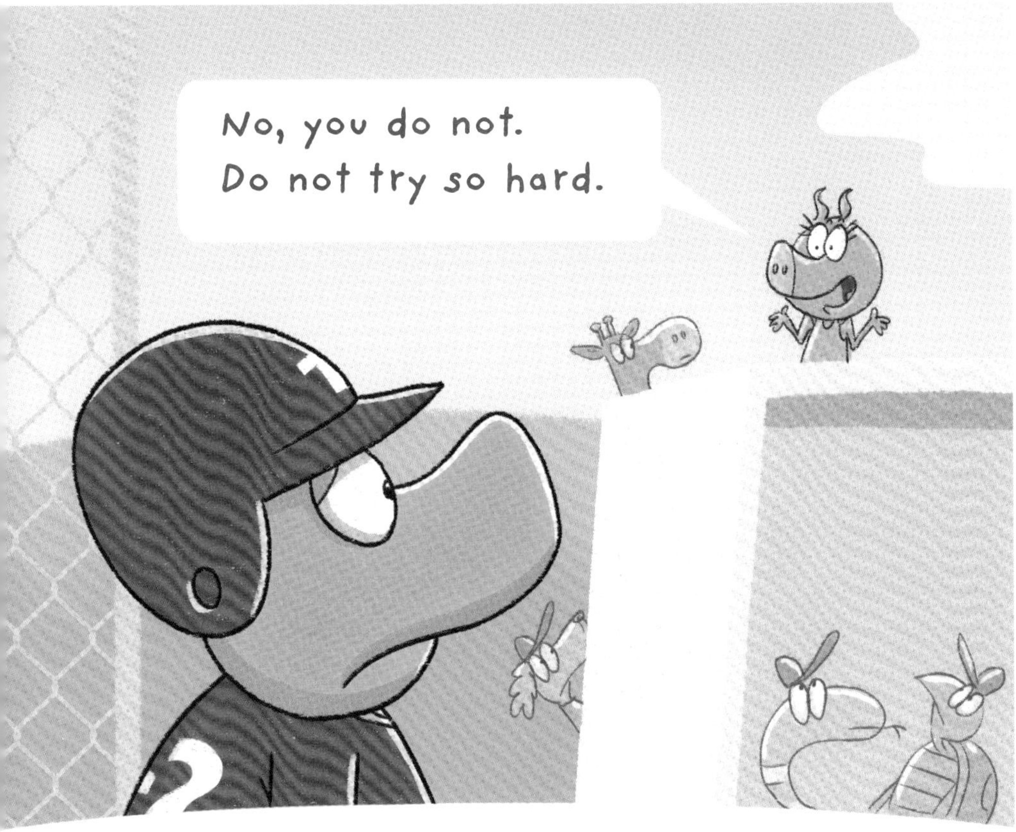
No, you do not.
Do not try so hard.

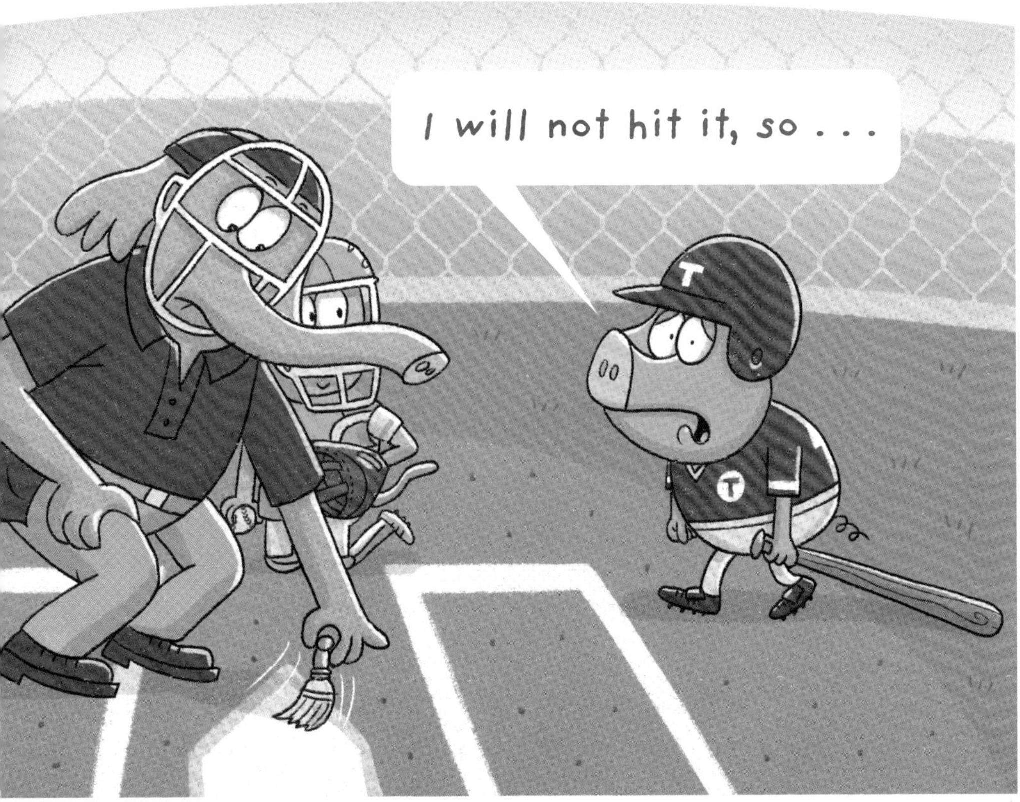
I will not hit it, so . . .

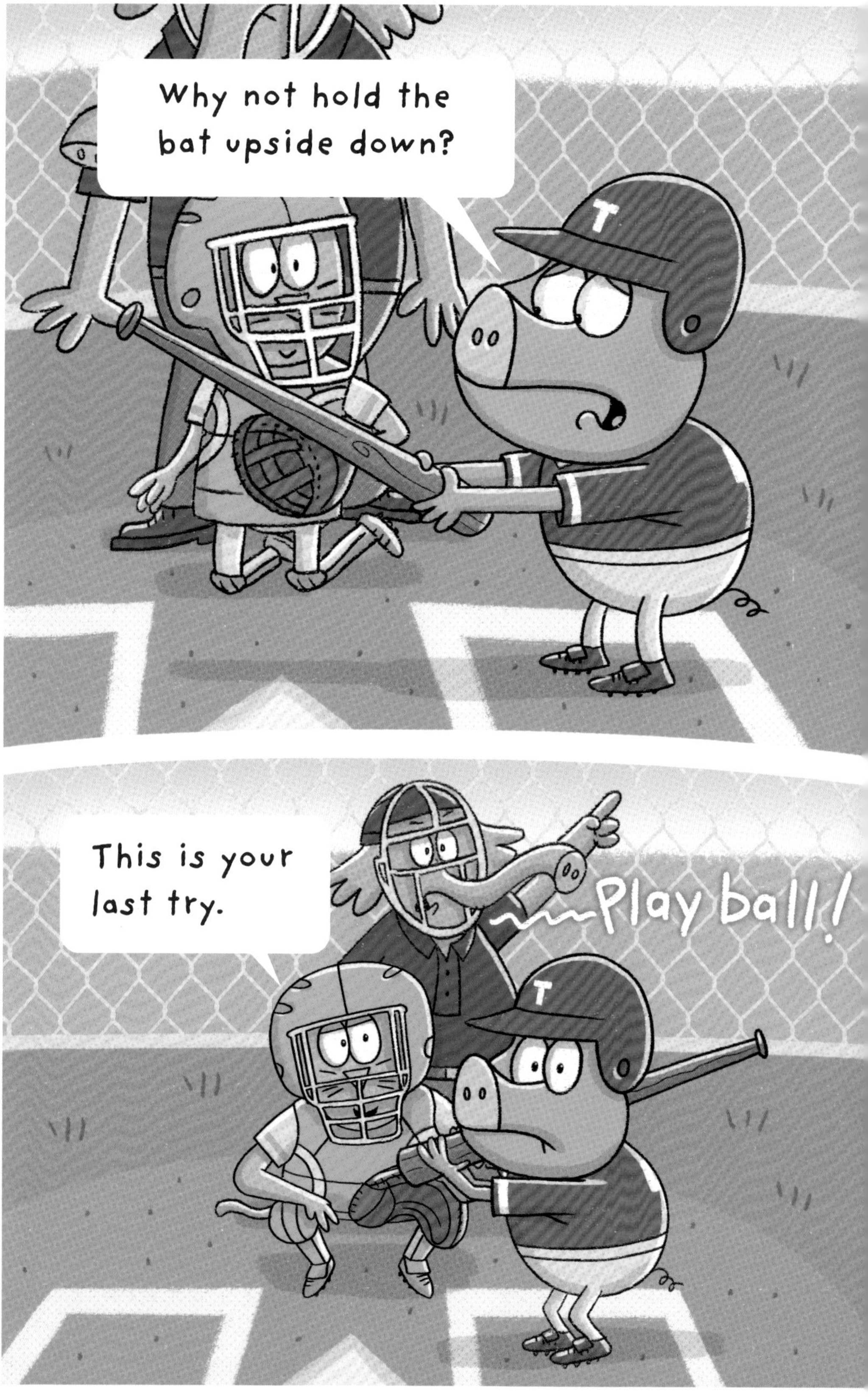
Why not hold the bat upside down?
This is your last try.
Play ball!

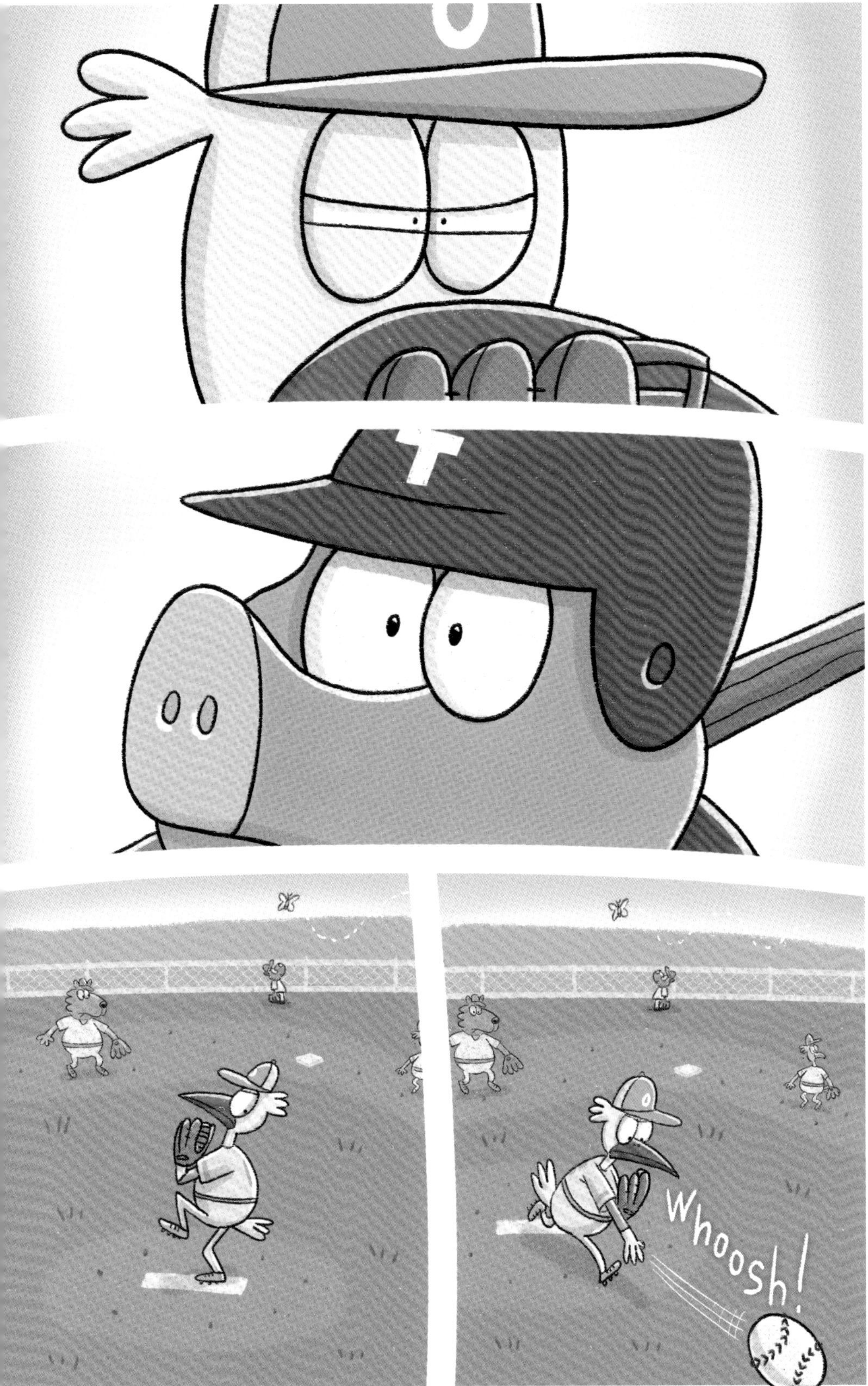
Whoosh!

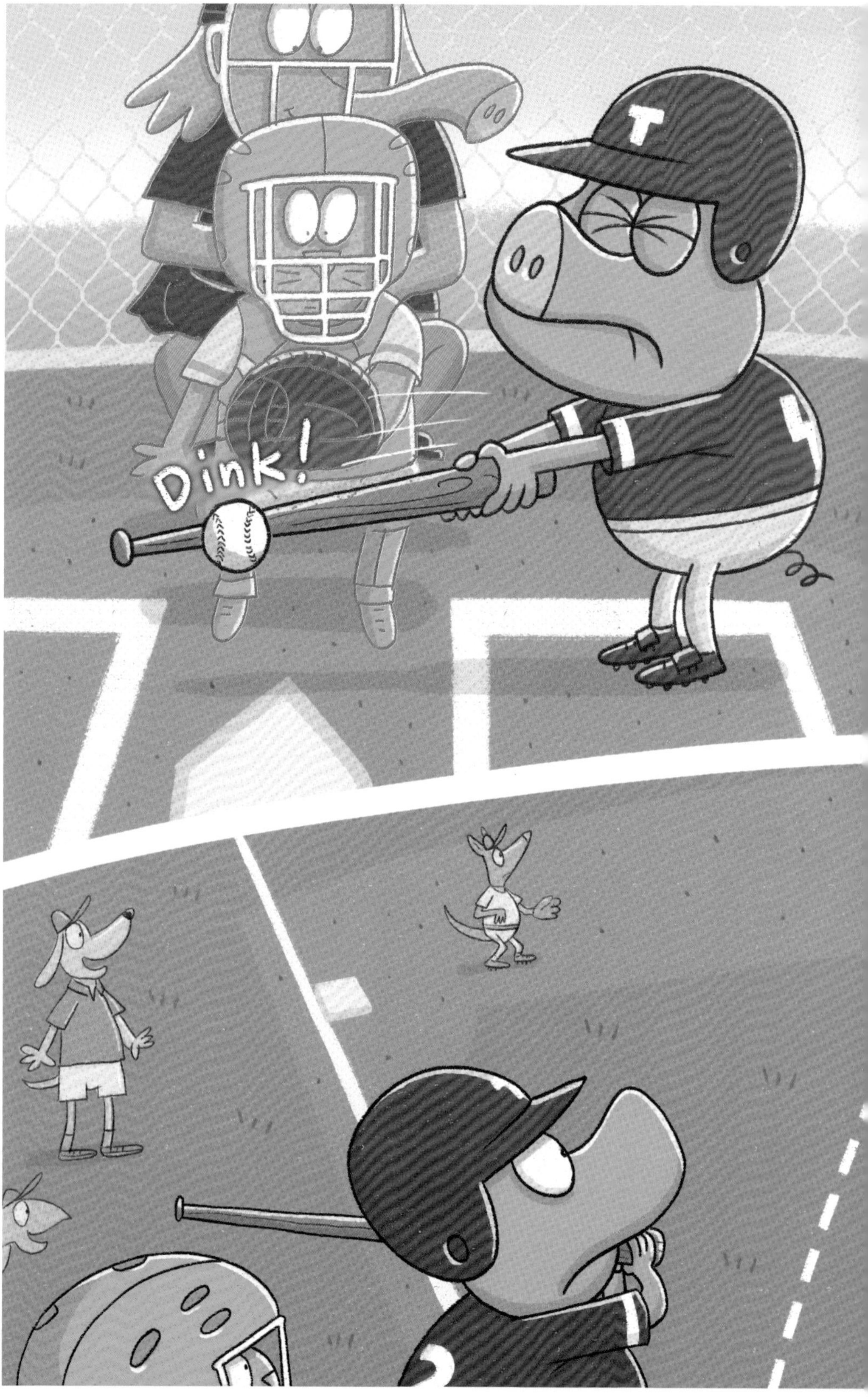
Dink!

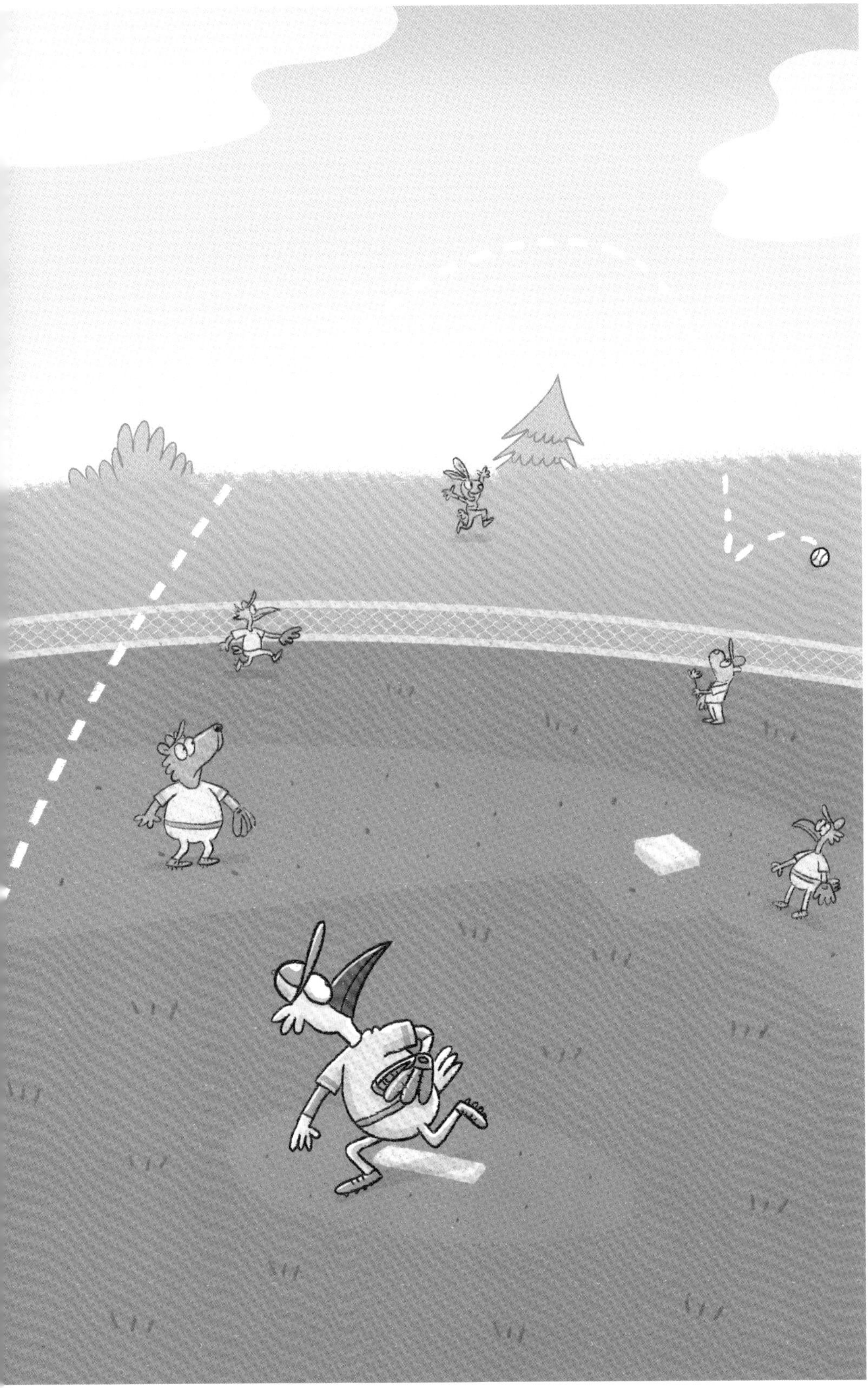

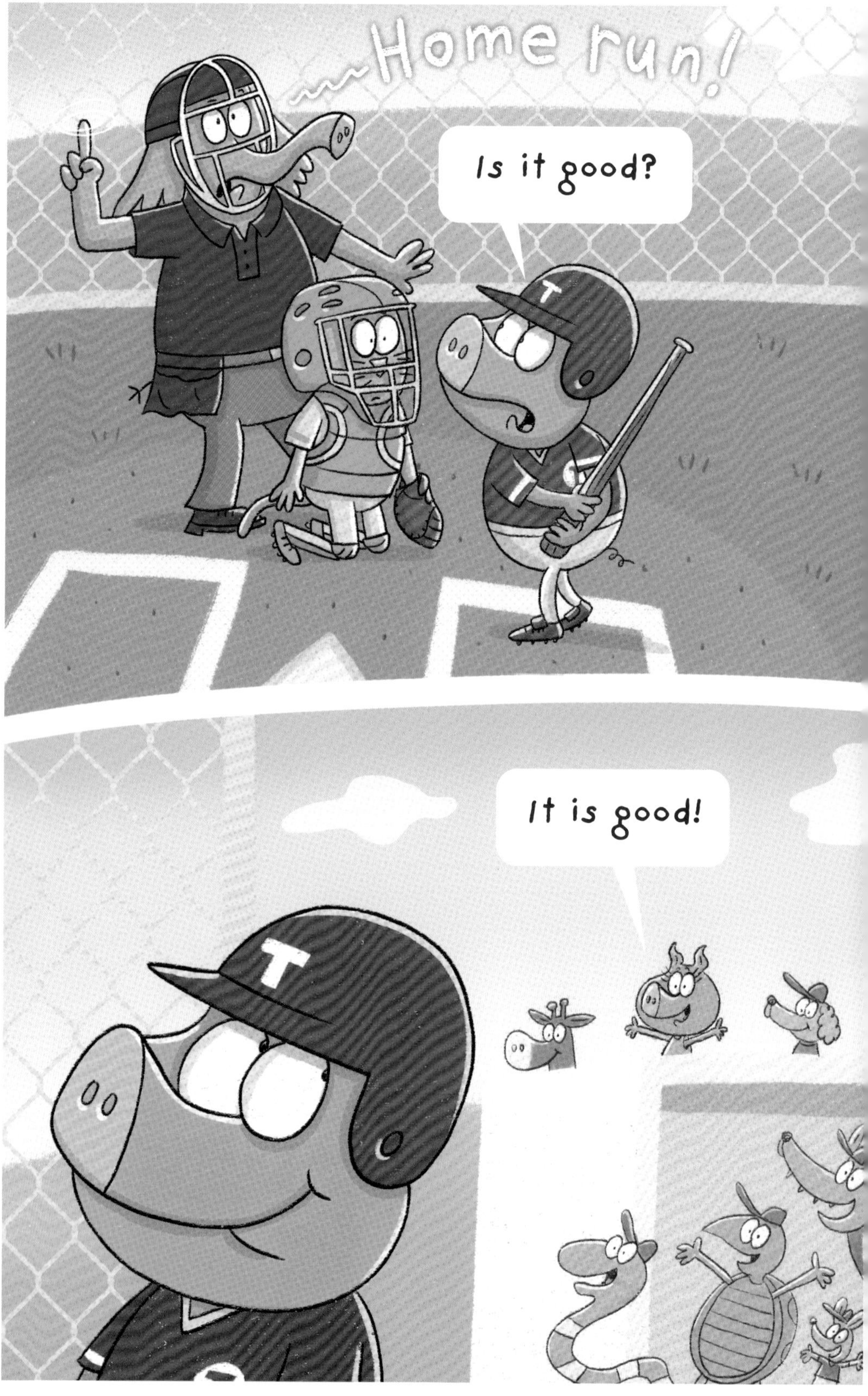
Home run!
Is it good?
It is good!

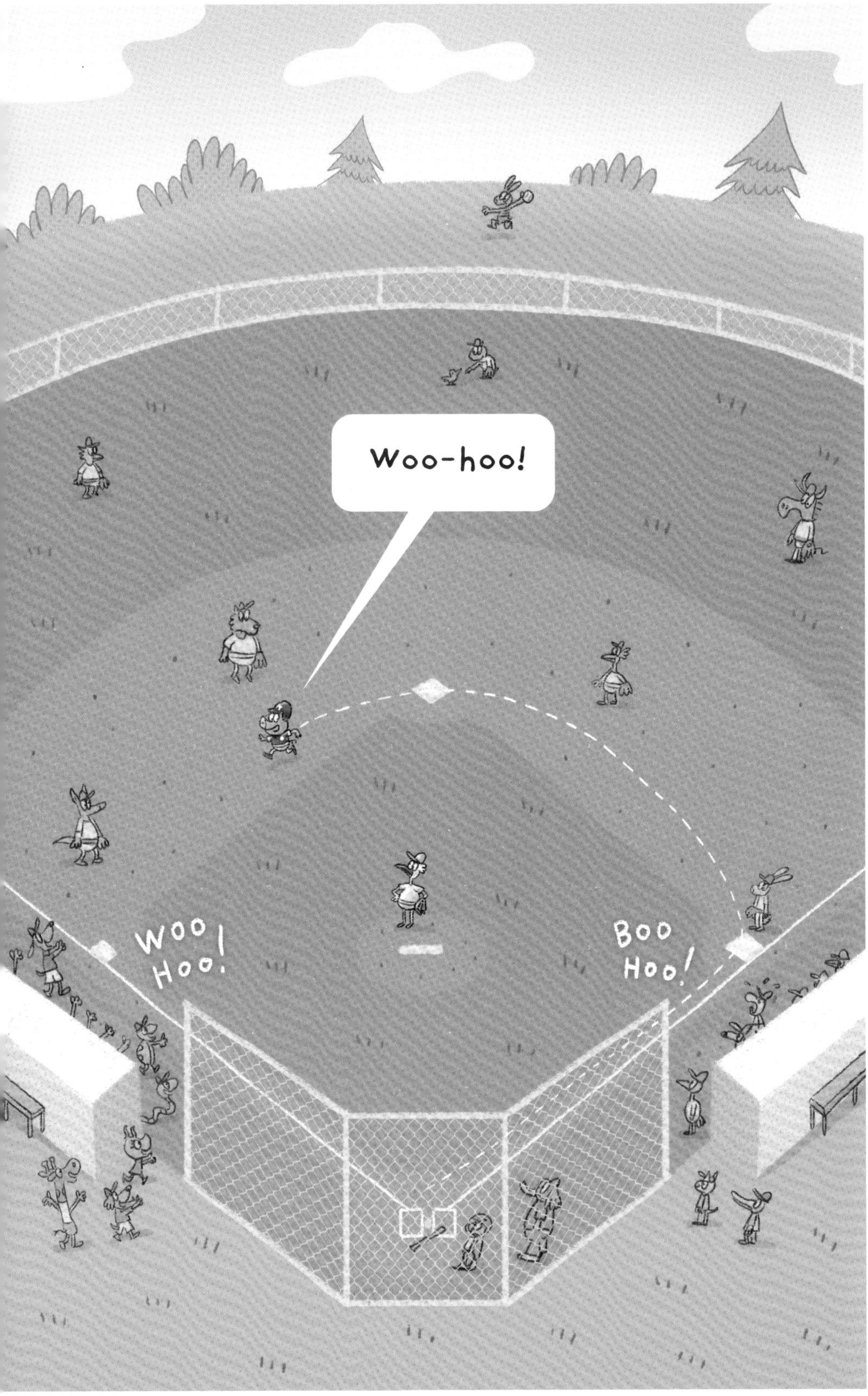

Woo-hoo!
Woo Hoo!
Boo Hoo!

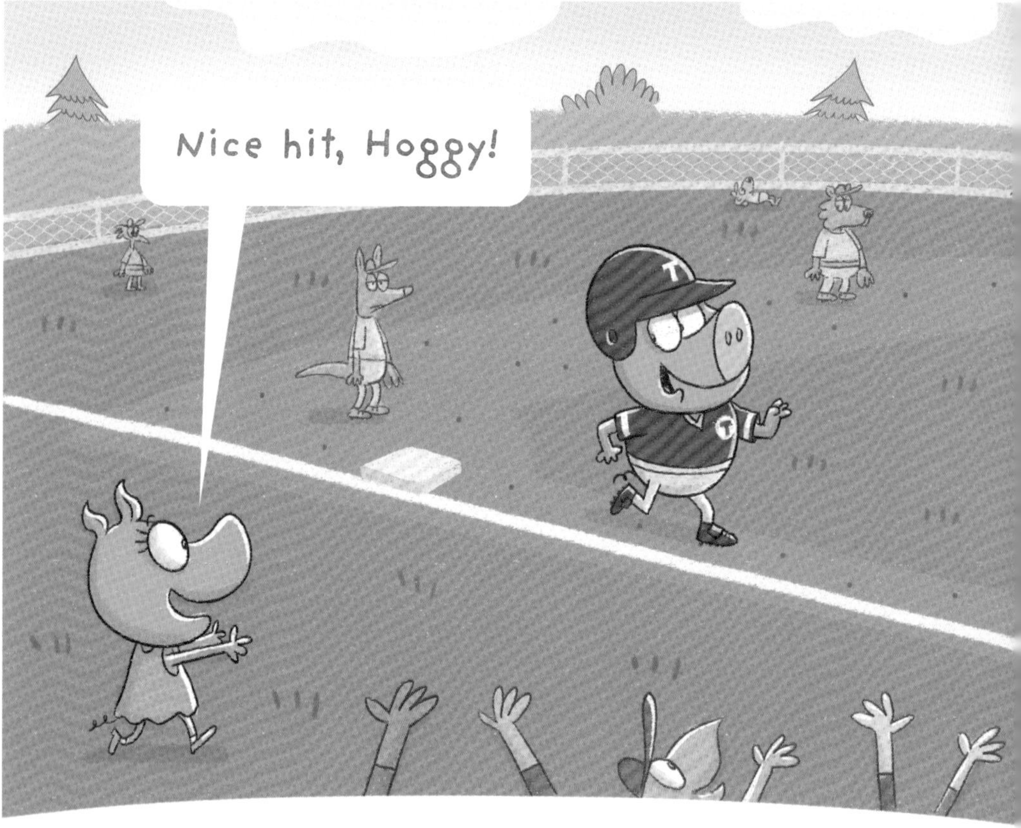
Nice hit, Hoggy!

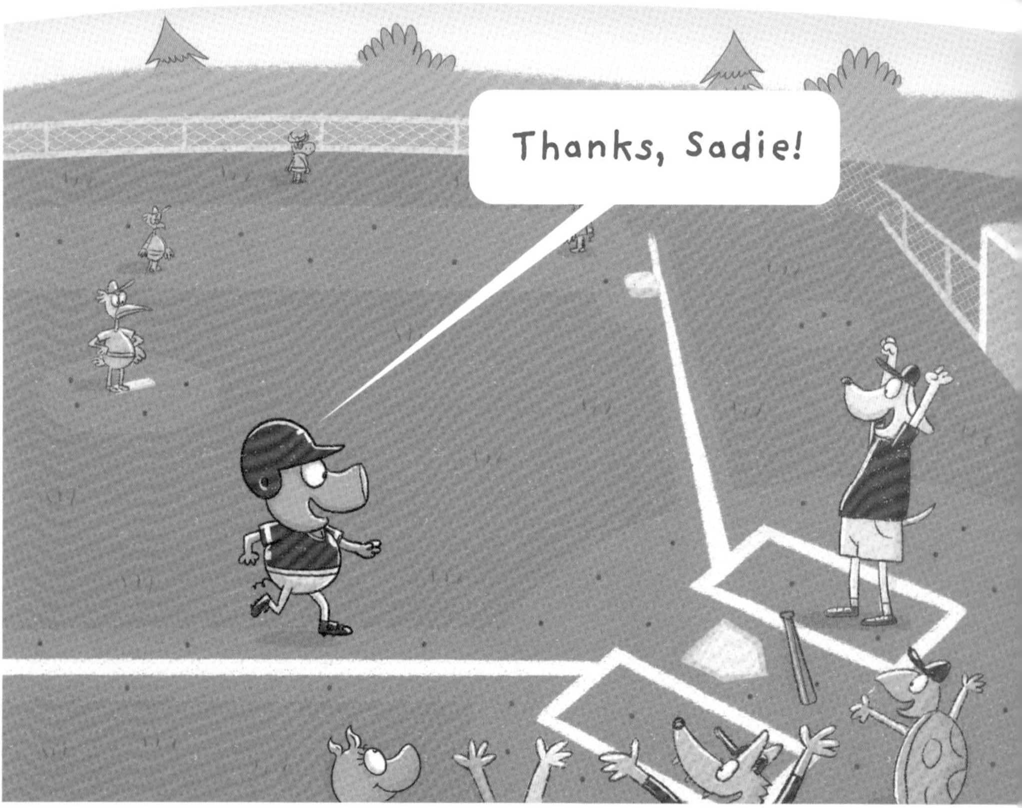
Thanks, Sadie!

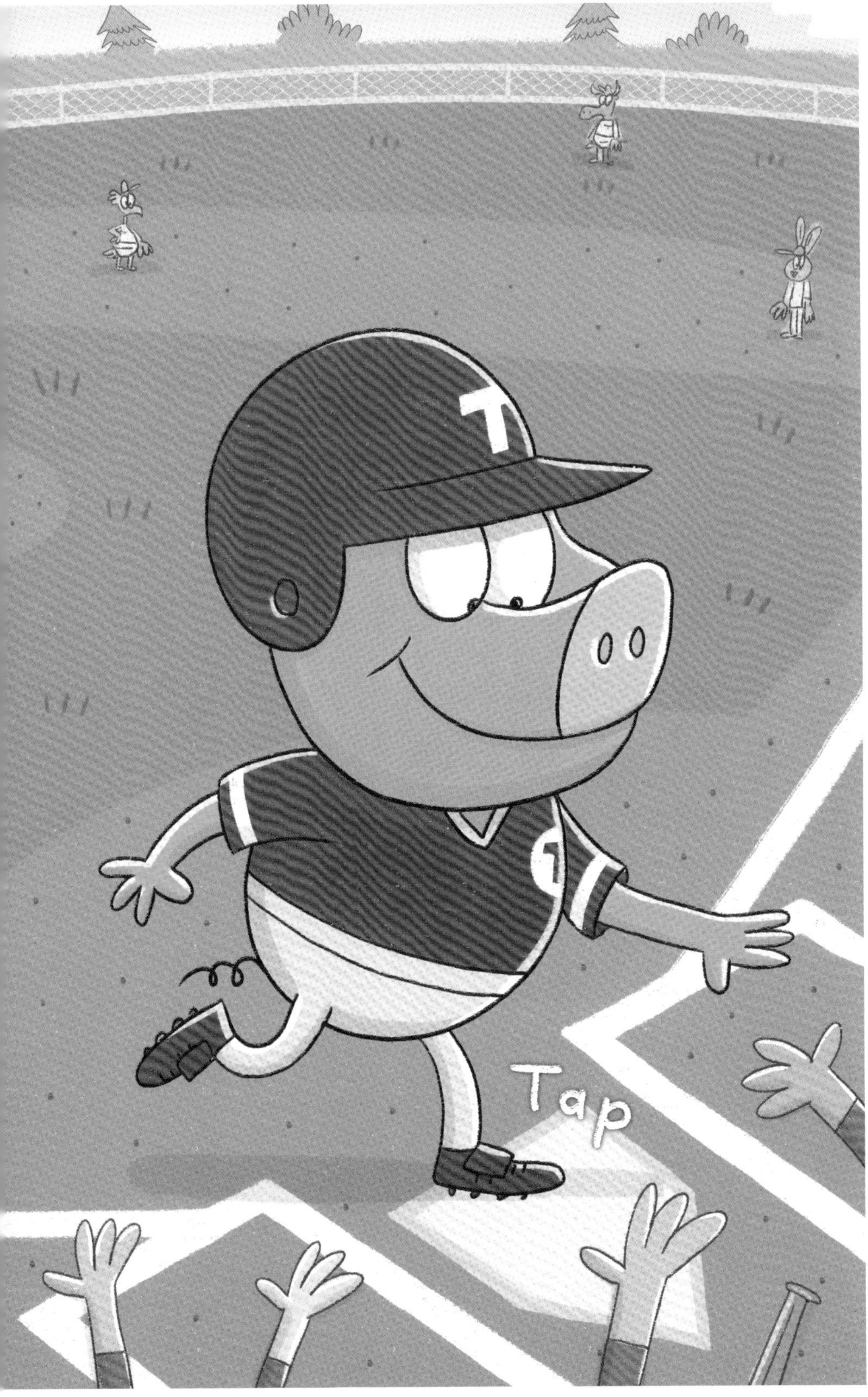
Tap

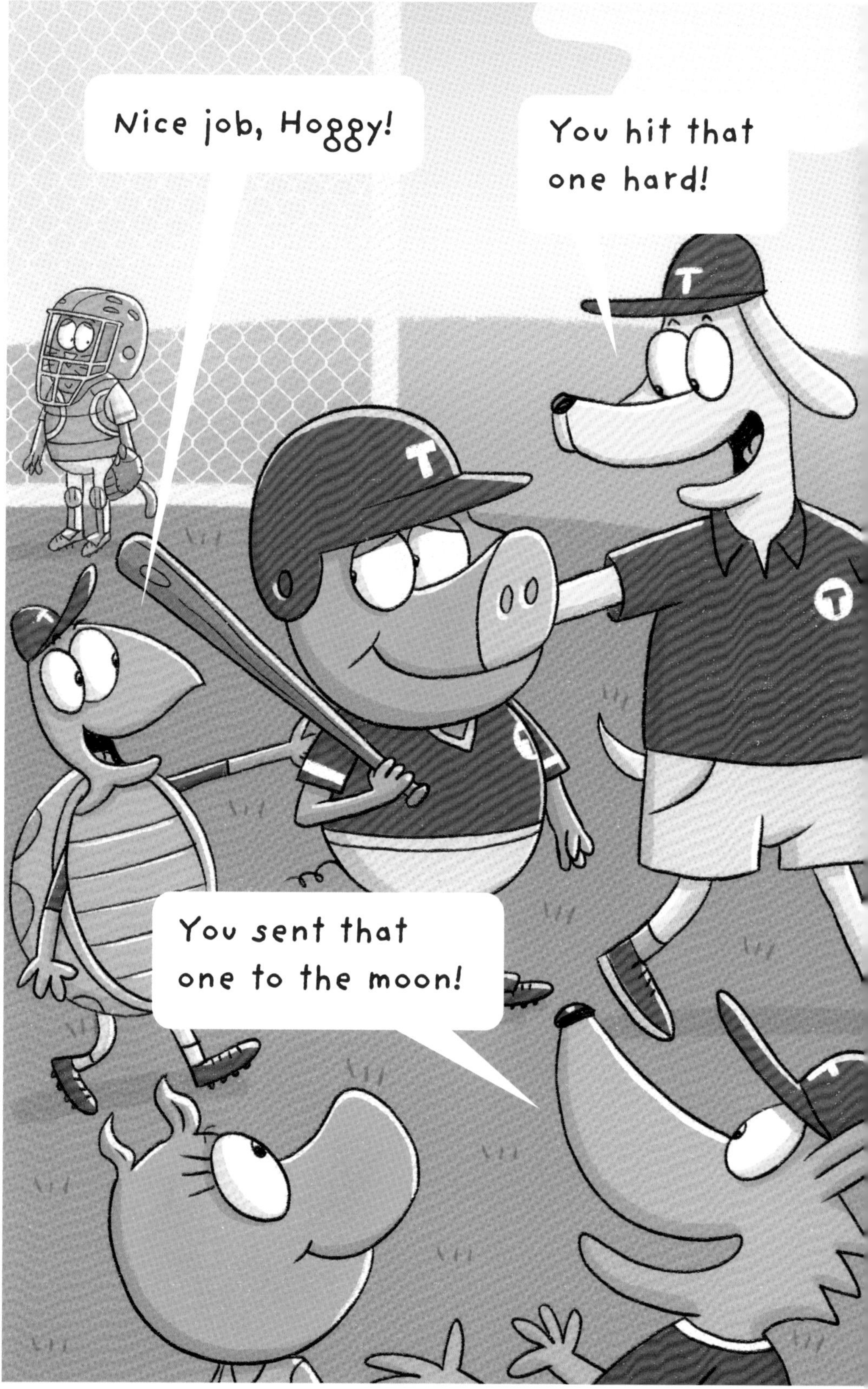
Nice job, Hoggy!
You hit that one hard!
You sent that one to the moon!

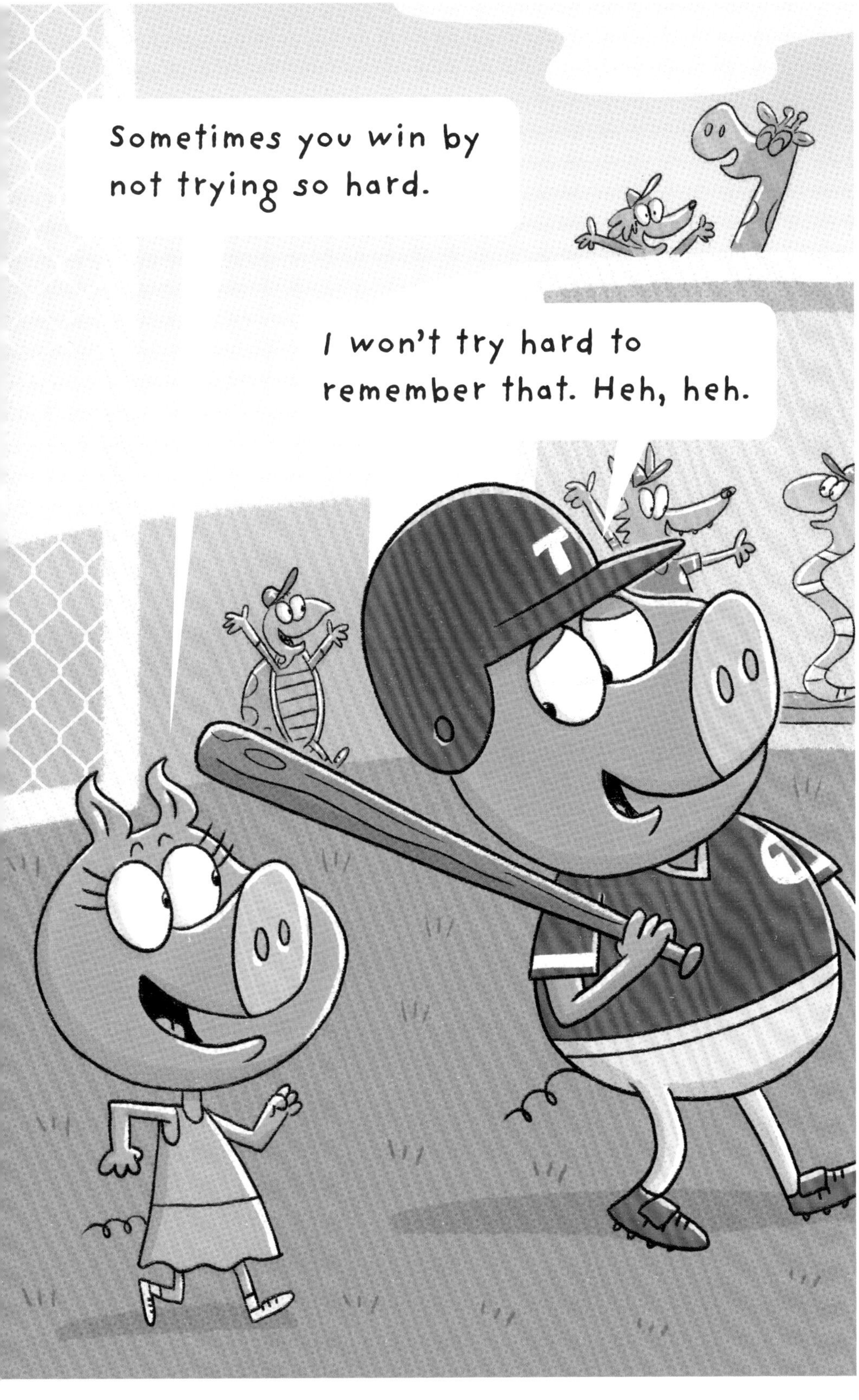
Sometimes you win by not trying so hard.
I won't try hard to remember that. Heh, heh.

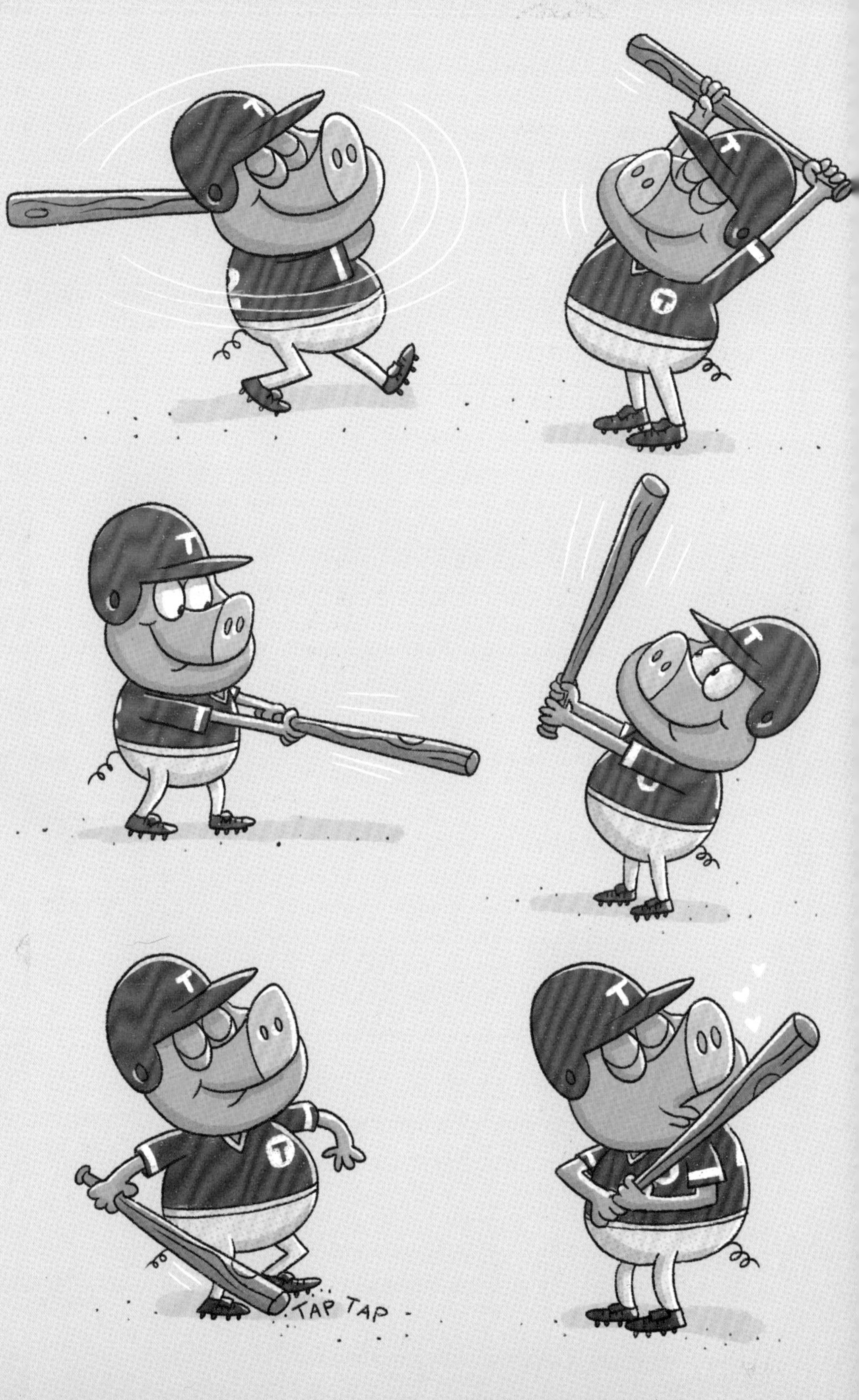
TAP TAP